The Plight
of Mattie Gordon

Sundowners
A division of
Treble Heart Books
1284 Overlook Dr.
Sierra Vista, AZ 85635-5512

Published and Printed in the U.S.A.

ISBN: 1-932695-47-8
ISBN: 9781932695472

All scriptures were taken from the King James Version of the Holy Bible, copyright 1984 by Thomas Nelson, Inc.

Thank you for choosing this compelling Inspirational Western from Sundowners and MountainView Publishing, a crossover novel

A crossover novel:

The Plight of Mattie Gordon

MountainView Publishing

and

Sundowners

Divisions

of

Treble Heart Books

Dedication

To my husband David. Thank you for showing me how to reach for my dreams. I love you as high as the sky.

Chapter One

The unmistakable sound of a rifle being cocked broke the stillness of the day. Mattie Gordon jumped out of her rocking chair and spun around to face the right side of the porch. Someone had aimed the double barrel of a rifle right between her eyes. She drew in a sharp breath and froze. Mattie had never been on the receiving end of a rifle before. Willing herself to look beyond the gun, she saw a black cowboy hat, rimming two of the darkest brown eyes she'd ever seen, narrowed directly at her.

"Put your hands up where I can see them." The deep masculine voice unnerved her as much as the rifle pointed at her.

She did as he commanded.

"Who are you?" the man growled.

Swallowing the lump in her throat, she forced herself to breathe normally. "I'm Mattie Gordon."

"Gordon?" She watched the man's eyes survey the surrounding porch and canyon floor as quick as a bolt of lightening flashes across the sky. "I'm looking for William Gordon. You his kin?"

"I'm his mother." Mattie squared her shoulders. "What do you want with Will?"

"You know when he'll be back?"

"He'll be back when his job is done and not a moment before."

"So, you admit he's on another job, huh?"

"Of course. My son is a hard working man."

Mattie didn't like the ugly, sinister expression of amusement, or the sound of his laughter mocking her. She put her hands down. "What do you want with Will?"

"Is there anyone else here?"

"No. They're all gone with Will on the trail drive." It never bothered Mattie to be alone. She enjoyed her leisure time when the boys were away. If this man would leave, she could get back to her needlepoint.

"Trail drive?" The man let down the gun a little, but still aimed it toward Mattie, every muscle in his body still alert and tense. "Is that what they call it?"

Mattie swiped some stray locks of blond hair out of her eyes and placed her hands on her hips. "Mr., you're getting me riled up. What's your business with my Will?"

The man kept his weapon ready for action and walked up onto the porch. Taking another look at her before he pushed open the door to the house, he aimed the rifle inside. He stepped into the little three-room cabin as cautiously as if it were overrun with newborn kittens.

Mattie watched him search her home from where she stood in the doorway, but she never moved from the porch. He came out of the house and proceeded to inspect the bunkhouse, small barn and outbuildings. When he returned, he eyed her curiously.

"You have any weaponry concealed on you?"

Mattie tilted her head back and laughed. The corners of his mouth curled up slightly.

"I had to ask." He shrugged his shoulders and gave her a sort of sideways grin.

"Why are you here? This is the last time I'm going to ask you. What business do you have with Will?"

He uncocked his rifle and reached into his black waistcoat pocket, produced a crumpled piece of paper, smudged with dirt, and handed it to her.

She unfolded it, and immediately recognized the hand-drawn likeness of her son. *Wanted. Cattle rustling, horse theft, murder. William Gordon. Three thousand dollar reward. Dead or alive.*

Mattie's knees gave out. She would have hit the floor if the man hadn't reached out and grasped her shoulders.

"Are you all right, Mrs. Gordon?"

Mattie felt as if all the air she'd ever breathed had been knocked out of her lungs with one of those sledgehammers she once saw the railroad workers sling. The man ran inside and returned with a dipper of water. He put the ladle to her lips and she drank. The liquid felt good going down her throat.

"This…" Her voice barely more than a whisper, she put her hand to her forehead to rub away the ache forming there. "This can't be right. My son is a good boy."

She looked into the stranger's eyes and saw something that hadn't been there before. Was it compassion? "You don't believe this, do you, Mr.?"

"Name's Braydon, ma'am." The man tipped his hat. "Cyrus Braydon. It's not for me to judge whether it's true or not."

"Then why are you looking for him?" Mattie helped herself to the rocking chair. Then with all the force of a locomotive, the realization of the man's purpose slammed her. She jumped to her feet and stared him in the eyes. "You're a bounty hunter, aren't you?"

Silence.

Mattie's breathing became shallow and rapid. She wanted to kick him and his calm resolve.

"Answer me!"

"Yes, I'm a bounty hunter."

Hot tears now stung her eyes and began rolling down her cheeks. "It's not true! Not one word of it! It's all lies!" She plopped backward into the rocking chair.

Mattie couldn't control her trembling. She buried her head in her hands and sobbed. The last time she cried like that was when her husband died of consumption twelve years ago, when she was thirty-four. Finally gaining control of herself, she looked for Mr. Braydon, but he was nowhere in sight. Neither was the ugly piece of paper that brought him here looking for her son.

Dear, sweet, gentle Will. He was a hired man, working for the biggest cattle barons in the western states. They hired him to run their stock to summer and winter pasture, from one state to another and out to the railroad in Hays, Kansas. He was a respected man among his peers. His hired men treated him with respect, as they did her. They would ride out whenever they had a job to do and be gone for as long as six weeks at a time, driving cattle for these rich men who paid well. Will and his bunch would return home, and she'd cook for them and look after them. They were all so happy.

She heard the horse before she saw Mr. Braydon round the corner, leading a dapple gray. He went to the corral, removed the saddle and tossed it to the ground with ease. Then he proceeded to remove the rest of the gear and let the horse loose. Mattie watched the whole thing in disbelief. His calm demeanor grated her.

He strode across the yard, kicking up little clouds of brown dust behind him.

"Surely you don't expect to stay here, Mr. Braydon?"

"How long ago did your son leave?"

"About two weeks ago." Why wouldn't he answer her questions? She inhaled deeply, attempting to calm herself.

"He'll be gone too long. Best I go out and meet him," he said more to himself than to Mattie. He climbed the stairs to the porch. "I'll bunk here for the night. It's been awhile since I've had a home-cooked meal and a nice, soft bed."

"You expect me to cook for you and bed you down?" Mattie's mouth dropped open.

His crooked smile appeared again, tightening a long scar on the right side of his chin. He stood a mere foot from her and tilted his head downward, staring directly into her eyes.

"Yup." The bounty hunter walked into her house, removed his hat and hung it on the peg by the door, as if he were the long-lost master come home from a tedious journey.

Mattie followed him with every intention of protesting. But she reminded herself this was not a nice man. He planned to take her son to jail—or worse. A man like Mr. Braydon was capable of anything. She sighed and resigned herself to not cross him during his stay.

Pulling the large frying pan down from the nail on the wall, she set it on the stove and poured some grease into it. Then she broke several eggs on the edge, dropped them in and a tossed a steak beside them. The bounty hunter didn't deserve such a grand meal, all compliments of Will Gordon. Mattie snickered to herself at the irony of it. Her son and his men provided lots of beef to keep them going all year long. They even dug a small icehouse out of the side of the canyon. Each winter they cut large blocks of ice from the frozen banks of the river to keep the meat cold. No. This man didn't deserve the fruits of her son's hard work.

"Supper's on," she said when she plunked plates of steaming food onto the table and poured two cups of coffee.

"Mm. Smells great." Mr. Braydon sat at the table across from Mattie and dug his fork into the eggs.

Mattie folded her hands before her and bowed her head. "Dear Lord, we ask that You would bless this food we are about to receive. Please bless Will as he works hard to take care of his mama. And bless Mr. Braydon, too. His misguided profession has brought him here for Your purpose. Please reveal that purpose to him. In Jesus' name, amen."

She looked up and saw Mr. Braydon watching her, his fork of eggs hovering above the plate.

"You really didn't know, did you?" His face softened for the first time since his unwanted arrival.

She didn't like the insinuation. That's she's naïve, maybe even a little stupid. If the poster was true, the last thing she wanted to do was let him think her son duped her. But had he?

Mattie chewed a small piece of steak without tasting it.

"I'm truly sorry, Mrs. Gordon. You seem like a nice lady. It's always sticky business meeting the kinfolk. Best not to run into them at all—especially the ones who don't know what their kin's been up to."

"Mr. Braydon, my son is not what you believe him to be. He runs an honest business."

"I'm sure that's what he's told you, ma'am. But I'm also sure that if you think about it hard enough, you'll be able to identify little clues pointing to him being on the wrong side of the law."

"No." She shook her head emphatically. "It's not possible."

They ate the rest of their meal in silence. Mattie cleaned up the dishes, retrieved her needlepoint from the porch, and sat in the tufted rocking chair by the fireplace.

"You've got a nice touch, Mrs. Gordon."

Mattie noticed him looking around the room, inspecting her pillows, wall hangings and tablecloth. She loved bringing colors into the little cabin. She did it to create a nice home for Will. Her son appreciated it, too. He told her so many times. He was a good son.

"I'm going to turn in now." Mr. Braydon stretched and yawned.

Fear shot through Mattie, but before she could voice it, he headed out the door. "The bunkhouse looks mighty inviting. Probably the cleanest, neatest one I've ever seen. Only a woman's touch could do that."

He took up his shotgun and covered his curly, dark brown hair with his hat. Turning in the doorway, he nodded to her.

"G'night, Mrs. Gordon."

She let out a sigh and stared after him. When he closed the door behind him, she made sure the bar was down tight, blew out the lamp, and went to bed fully clothed.

Mattie barely slept, her thoughts kept her awake. Throughout the night she weighed the situation. She couldn't believe her son capable of the things listed on the wanted poster. Especially murder.

The words of the stranger seeped into her mind. *I'm sure if you think about it hard enough, you'll be able to identify little clues, pointing to him being on the wrong side of the law.* Were there such signs?

Will and all his men were very good with their handguns. They practiced for hours each day. That wasn't so unusual. All men loved shooting, didn't they? Will told her they needed to keep sharp for when they encounter danger along the trail. Snakes and mountain lions and wild things were a constant threat to both men and cattle.

Mattie paused. Mountain lions? In Texas, Oklahoma and Kansas? She'd traveled through these territories and states when they moved to the hidden canyon in the flatlands of Colorado. Not a mountain to be seen, nor a lion. She shook her head. This didn't mean a thing. Mr. Braydon was trying to make her believe her son capable of unspeakable things.

She rose early and went outside to the outhouse, then drew

fresh water from the well for the day. Mattie carried the water bucket into the house. She took up her egg basket and headed for the coop. Feeding the chickens gave her pleasure. She liked her chickens. Will bought them for her so the men and she could have an endless supply of eggs and fried chicken. While the fowl pecked for their breakfast, she hunted eggs.

The men were always doing nice things for her, so it was no trouble for her to show her appreciation by keeping them well fed and happy. They'd all been together for years now. Not one of them ever left, except for Jim. He met a pretty girl while they were in Oklahoma last year, and he hadn't returned with the rest of them. Mattie would have liked to say goodbye to Jim. She liked him. Why hadn't he ever written to them? He told her she was like family to him. An ugly thought suddenly came to her. Were they really like family, or more like a *gang*? *No*. She mustn't think that way.

It's that bounty hunter's fault. She despised him for putting these doubts into her head about her boy. She raised Will to be a good man. It had been hard, but from an early age he'd provided for her.

Returning to her kitchen, she stirred a batch of biscuits, then pounded out her frustrations on the dough. How? How had a boy of thirteen been capable of making that kind of money when her husband hadn't been able of doing it? It was impossible for him to have been a law-breaker back then, and just as implausible that he's now twenty-five years old.

Struggling with her thoughts, she pushed the pan of perfectly cut biscuits into the oven and slammed the door. Then she put on some bacon and eggs to fry, and soon the little cabin was filled with delicious aromas.

Mr. Braydon knocked on the door and entered the huge front room that extended the full length of the front of the cabin.

"Nice of you to knock," she said over her shoulder.

"I knew you were up. I could smell the food from the corral." He hung his hat, stowed his rifle, and pulled up a chair at the long table.

"Are you planning on riding out today?"

"As soon as I'm through with my breakfast."

Mattie nodded in satisfaction. The sooner she fed him, the sooner she'd be rid of him.

They ate in silence.

She washed the dishes while Mr. Braydon prepared his horses to leave, one for riding and one for carrying dirty bags of what she figured contained personal belongings. When she finished her chore, she went out onto the porch and watched him lead both of his horses out of the corral. He mounted and rode to the cabin, pulling his packhorse behind him, and tipped his hat to her.

As if a man like that could have manners.

"Thank you, Mrs. Gordon. I appreciate your hospitality."

Hospitality? He'd given her no choice.

He leaned forward in his saddle. "I wish we could have met under more pleasant circumstances. Good day to you." He rode past the house and headed through the only exit in the narrow canyon.

Mattie walked to the other side of the house and watched him go. Her keen eyes scanned the steep, walls of the gorge. The jagged rocks, all with fault lines, which often hid spires of rocks in an illusion of being one solid wall, never ceased to amaze her. They were hidden away from the rest of the world there. No one had ever entered their canyon home before Mr. Braydon, other than Will and his men. And Mattie. Will told her she would be safe there when he and the men went to work. No one would be able to find her. It put his mind at ease to know she was safe.

Why did she need to be safe? From what? Or whom? People like Mr. Braydon? Her eyes rested on the spot where one of the men always stood guard. No one would ever know anyone was there. The perfect hiding spot. Why did they feel it necessary to guard the canyon entrance? She'd questioned her son about it once, and he mumbled something about not wanting robbers, who might know they had fresh earnings in their pokes, to enter.

Mr. Braydon rounded the curve in the canyon, disappearing from her view. Along with the extra biscuits and hardtack he took, he also stole all her innocent ideas about her son.

The poster read, *Dead or Alive.* The reality hit her like a boulder falling from the canyon. Mr. Braydon was after her son, and nothing would stop him from collecting the reward. Nothing. Whether she believed her son innocent or guilty, she was obligated to warn him.

Mattie spurred into action. She packed a bedroll, a change of clothes, and plenty of food and water. Having done this for her son countless times before, her work went quickly.

She saddled her horse, secured her provisions, and mounted. Taking mental inventory of everything she needed, she knew she hadn't forgotten anything. When her gaze rested on the chicken coop, she made a mental note to stop at the nearest ranch and make arrangements for Mr. Rance to take care of her chickens while she was away.

"Lord, please help me. All I ask is that you guide Midnight's steps, and give me at least one more chance to tell Will about You."

Mattie reined her horse toward the canyon mouth, leaving all comfort and safety behind her, her only focus to get to Will before that bounty hunter.

Chapter Two

Cyrus stretched out sideways on his wool blanket, leaning an elbow against his saddle. He sipped his coffee and poked at the fire with a scrub oak branch. Knowing the Gordon gang wouldn't be headed his direction for several weeks, he relaxed for the first time since discovering their trail. Where would be the best place to wait for the notorious outlaw? The canyon hideaway would mean certain death. His trained eyes noted the rock outcroppings big enough to hide a man.

Yet, there on the floor of the prairie, he was exposed to the world. *Choose your own ground to fight.* The words of his mentor, Sheriff Craig Wilson, never failed him. Cyrus decided to continue tracking Will Gordon and his gang.

Through the gentle, evening breeze, his keen ears heard a snap. Remaining motionless, he slowly reached for his rifle and cocked it. Another noise. Squinting straight ahead through the fire, he focused on a shadowy figure on a horse moving toward him.

"That's close enough, Partner. Identify yourself or be shot."

"It's Mattie Gordon."

Cyrus didn't remember his mouth dropping open, but he suddenly realized it needed to be closed. "What are you doing here?" He uncocked his rifle and stood.

Mattie pulled up, dismounted, and ground tied the horse he'd seen in the canyon corral. She walked directly up to the fire and warmed herself. "I've come to persuade you to not turn my boy in to the authorities."

Cyrus laughed. "Ma'am. I can't do that. He's a lawless man and justice needs to be served."

"But you don't know for sure if he's guilty." Mattie glared at him, her blue eyes dark and accusing. The glow of the fire danced across her tanned face and caused her dark blond hair to shimmer with golden flecks. She stood no more than five feet tall, yet Cyrus instinctively knew she aimed to get what she wanted.

"That's right. But there are plenty of eyewitnesses who'll testify against him and his gang. They've been caught red-handed several times, but they're slipperier than a frog in a rainstorm." He put his rifle down and sat on his blanket. "I'm only doing the law a favor by helping them find Will and bring him in."

"But the poster said *dead or alive*. What if something happens to him and he never gets the chance at a fair trial? Maybe he's innocent."

"Ma'am. That's not for me to say. It's up to a jury and judge to decide. My job is to find him and bring him in." He sipped his coffee. Now cold, he tossed it onto the ground. "I'm going to get some sleep. You're welcome to my fire tonight. Then tomorrow at first light, you're going back home where you belong."

He lay back against his saddle, pulled the blanket around himself and closed his eyes. Maybe she'd get the hint and do the same. Better yet, maybe she'd go home.

Cyrus heard rustling around the campfire, and knew Mattie prepared to settle in for the night. He didn't know why, but he took comfort in having someone share his camp. Through the years, he'd come across several family members of the men he hunted. They all acted the same, either maintaining their loved ones' innocence, or trying to persuade him not to do his job.

This little lady didn't know who she was up against. Cyrus prided himself in being a seasoned bounty hunter. Everyone knew they could count on him to bring in the right man. He only shot a few and wounded them; none died by his hand. That brought comfort to him. Maybe it shouldn't. He cared about these varmints as if they weren't despicable outlaws. He hated that part of himself. *Besides, real human beings don't treat others like Will Gordon does.*

The next thing Cyrus knew, the dawn of a new day warmed his face. He opened his eyes and stretched his arms high above his head. Looking across the fire ring, he saw a sleeping form. She hadn't gone home yet? He'd see to it right after breakfast.

He got up and walked around the smoldering campfire to get the kinks out of his tired limbs, a routine he'd done every morning for over twenty years. Finding privacy to take care of his personal needs proved a challenge. There wasn't much more than prairie grasses in this huge, open land. He used his horse to screen him from the sleeping woman.

Cyrus brought out his frying pan and soon had slabs of salt bacon sizzling over a small fire. Then he placed the biscuits he took from Mattie's house to warm on the rocks ringing the fire.

She groaned and rolled onto her back. Sleepy, blue eyes peeked out from under the blanket.

"Mornin'," Cyrus said, glad she was finally up and would soon be gone.

"Good morning." She sat up and pushed the blanket back. "Smells good."

"Yup. Eats good, too."

Mattie folded her blanket and straightened her skirt, as if

trying to brush the wrinkles out. Cyrus mused that there was no one out here to try to impress, yet she continued to work at fixing herself up as if she were going to town on a shopping spree.

"Food's done."

He dished up some breakfast onto his only plate and gave it to Mattie, eating his portion directly from the pan. While Cyrus cleaned the dishes, Mattie saddled her horse and tied everything back onto her saddle.

"I need privacy," she announced.

"I'll turn my back."

"That's not good enough." Her blue eyes narrowed at him and became gray as storm clouds.

"It's going to have to be enough," he snapped. "There aren't any trees out here."

Mattie looked around the meager campsite. "I'll have to rig a blanket up over my horse and use that."

"That'll take too much time. I'll look away."

Ignoring him, she draped a blanket over her horse, allowing it to touch the ground. Then she disappeared behind it for a few moments. By the time she finished, Cyrus had his own horses saddled and ready to go.

"Good luck to you, ma'am." He tipped his hat and turned his mount northeast.

"Thanks, but I'm going with you."

Cyrus stopped and turned to stare at the woman. "You're *not* coming with me, and that's final. Now, go home, woman."

She pulled her horse up beside his and glared at him. "I'm going with you to make sure you don't shoot my son, and that's *final.*"

Cyrus sat straight in the saddle. He sighed and clamped his jaw tight. How could he get rid of her? He took his rifle out of its leather boot and dismounted. Striding over to her, he raised it and aimed at her head.

"Look, Mrs. Gordon. You're not invited to come with me." He cocked the rifle. "If you don't turn around now and go home, I'll have no choice but to stop you with whatever means I have available to me."

"You're not going to shoot me, Mr. Braydon." Her soft, gentle voice grated on his nerves.

"What makes you think I won't?"

"Because, regardless of what I think of you as a bounty hunter, I can see that underneath your rough exterior beats the heart of a man who has respect for the law."

He lowered his rifle. She wasn't the first person to tell him that, and it infuriated him. "If I can't stop you, I can slow you down long enough for you to not be able to find me."

She leaned toward him. "What you don't know is that Will told me how to get a hold of him if I ever need him." She shifted in the saddle and straightened her back. "Regardless of whatever laws you believe he might be breaking, I know down in my heart that my son is a good man."

Cyrus hadn't thought of that. If she knew where Will was, it would save him weeks of tracking. But could he trust her? What would a mother do to save her young'un? He'd seen and heard it all before. Why would this lady be any different? No, he'd have to trust his own instincts, not some pretty little widow woman. "I'll take my chances alone. If you follow me, I'll have to shoot your horse, and don't think I won't." He pointed a finger at her and watched the look on her face fade to one of defeat. Good. Now maybe she'd leave him alone.

Without a word, Mattie turned her horse and headed southeast. Cyrus watched her until he was certain she wasn't going to follow him. He mounted his horse and rode northeast.

Cyrus made good time, and only stopped to munch on hardtack and biscuits when his horse needed a rest. During one of these breaks, he found his mind wandering to Mattie Gordon. He then realized she hadn't headed west, toward home. Southeast. Why? Had she told the truth? Did she really know where Will would be? If so, she would arrive before him, tip the Gordon gang off, and by the time Cyrus arrived, there would be no trace of any of them.

He furrowed his brows. Now what should he do? Turn around and follow her? What if she was bluffing? He kicked the dirt with his boot. He'd never been confused by a kin before. Breathing deeply, he looked to the sky for the answer. *Always rely on your own instincts.* The good sheriff's wisdom came through for him when he needed it.

He continued traveling northeast.

Mattie knew she would find Will before the bounty hunter. He was heading in the wrong direction. While she did want to confront her son with the accusations printed on the wanted poster, she also wanted justice to be served. Her mother's heart broke at the thought of Will serving a lifetime in jail.

She knew her son wasn't ready to meet eternity, having spoken to him about his soul several times. He dismissed it as being silly, female religion. If she could get to him before Cyrus, she could have one more chance at bringing him to a place where he would ask God's forgiveness for his sins.

Mattie wished Cyrus would be there when it happened. It would be easier to give Will up than to try to talk him into giving himself up. Oh, how had this happened? How could the things listed on the wanted poster be true?

She stopped by a stream to rest a while. Kneeling at the water's edge, she scooped some of the cool, clear water into her hands and drank. It refreshed her. She lay on her back and looked up at the sky. *Lord, why have You forsaken me? The only way out of this mess is to find Will before Cyrus. Help me prepare my son's heart for what I have to say to him about his soul. Please keep him safe. I give my boy into Your hands, Lord. Have Your way in his life. In the name of Jesus. Amen.*

Mattie pushed on toward Boise City, Oklahoma, and arrived two days later. All along the trail she thought about what Cyrus told her, that she could identify things to confirm what the poster said about Will.

This was one of those times. Will often told her if anything ever happened and she needed to find him, to go to Boise City and send a telegram from there to Doc Lundine in Hays, Kansas. He'd drilled her to make sure she memorized each word. Regardless of what the problem was, the message would be the same. She spoke the words aloud to her horse. "Doc Lundine, my boy is very ill and in need of attention. Please advise as soon as possible. Mrs. Gordon."

Will told her Dr. Lundine would know exactly how to reach him, and she must be patient and wait for him at the hotel. It could take several days to get the message to him.

Although she memorized it long ago, Mattie now wondered why she wasn't allowed to use Will's name. Why say he was ill, when he's not? She knew it was some sort of code, but until now she hadn't given it much thought. If it brought Will to her safely, she'd use it.

Arriving in Boise City, she first sent the telegram, then went to the hotel and rented a room. Money was no problem. Her son provided for her well. Living in the canyon all those years, she saved quite a bit and might as well use some of it now.

The days in Oklahoma passed slowly for Mattie. She purchased a few items that could be carried on horseback, treated herself to long walks, and dined in the only restaurant in town. Without having any housework or cooking to do, she grew restless.

She even visited the local preacher to ask his advice about

Will. She never mentioned her son's name, nor told him the extent of the boy's sins. But talking about it gave her the confidence. When she found her son, she'd tell him about Jesus and how He died for him for the forgiveness of his sins. She'd encourage him to turn himself in to be held accountable for his wrongdoings. But if he didn't, would she have the strength to turn her only son over to the authorities? She reminded herself of how God turned his only son over to the authorities, innocent of all crimes the mob accused him of. Mattie smiled. God understood her dilemma. He would give her what she needed to accomplish whatever had to be done.

After six days, Mattie began to wonder if her son was still alive. Had Cyrus found him first? She paced the floor of her hotel room, wondering how much longer she could stand to wait and pray.

A knock on her door startled her. She rushed to open it. A boy about fifteen years old stood before her.

"Are you Mrs. Gordon?"

"Yes. That's me."

"I have a telegram for you." He held out an envelope for her to take. Then he handed her a notebook. "Please sign here."

Mattie signed her name and closed the door behind her, locking it. With trembling hands, she opened the envelope and extracted a small, folded piece of paper.

Mrs. Gordon, son will be fine. Take him to Liberal, Kansas, in one week for a checkup. Doc Lundine.

More code? It appeared that she was to meet Will in Liberal one week from today. Not knowing how to get there, she needed to get directions. Tucking the missive into her pocket, she unlocked the door and stepped into the hallway. She bumped into a person. The impact of the muscular chest sent her reeling backward. Strong arms grabbed her and kept her from falling onto the floor.

"Are you all right, ma'am?"

Mattie's head jerked up. She looked into the tanned face of Cyrus Braydon.

"You?" He thrust her back onto her feet and scowled. Mattie thought his rugged features suited the bounty hunter in him. Maybe he looked halfway presentable underneath those unkempt whiskers.

"Have you found Will yet?" She hoped he'd give her the right answer.

"No. Have you?"

Mattie sighed and gazed downward toward the carpeted floor of the hotel hallway. Why did she feel disappointed to know her son hadn't been caught yet? Wasn't that what she hoped he'd tell her?

"I didn't figure you had. I'm surprised you haven't given up and gone home. It takes a professional to track down a man."

Mattie laughed. "A professional like you? It took you a week and a half longer to get as far as I did in three days."

Cyrus narrowed his eyes, but didn't say anything for a moment.

She raised her head and looked down the hallway. This confrontation was getting her nowhere. "Excuse me, please. I wish to pass."

He stepped aside and Mattie strode past. As she was about to turn the corner and go down the stairs, Cyrus called to her.

"Mrs. Gordon."

She turned back. "Yes, Mr. Braydon?"

"Since it looks like we're both staying here for the night, would you like to join me for supper?"

Mattie took in a sharp breath. Should she? After all, he was the enemy. No. That's not right. The enemy was the evil one who had pulled her only son into a lawless state. The evil one who was trying to destroy him. This man was only that, a man.

"Sure," she replied. "Why not?"

He smiled. Mattie thought it was a nice smile. "How about seven?" he suggested.

She nodded. "Seven sounds fine."

He tipped his hat, and she left him standing in the hallway. She asked the hotel manager if he knew how to get to Liberal, Kansas. He didn't, but suggested she check with the Bureau of Land Management. It was in a two-story building designed for nothing but offices. Mattie entered and walked up to a young lady sitting behind a mahogany desk. Her skin looked smooth as the porcelain doll her mother once gave her for Christmas. She remembered her own face and hands having the same qualities once, over twenty years ago. The lady directed her to an agency up the stairs.

Once there, Mattie breathed deeply and knocked on the office door.

A man's tenor voice called, "Come in."

She entered the room and a string bean of a man stepped from behind his desk, bony hand extended. "Welcome, ma'am. Come on in and sit down." He directed Mattie to a worn, but comfortable leather chair.

"Now, what can I do for you?"

"I've been told you would be able to tell me how to get to Liberal, Kansas."

"Yes, ma'am. I could tell you that, but why don't you take the stage?" He laughed, then snorted. "Were you planning on going by buggy? Do you have someone to chaperone you?" The man leaned forward, a look of interest on his face.

Mr., you'd be the last person on earth I'd ask to chaperone me. "Actually, I planned on riding there by horseback."

The man's mouth fell open. Mattie struggled to keep from snickering. His mouth stretched much farther than any she'd seen before. *I wonder if a bear lives in that cave?*

"You can't be serious? Alone?"

"Sir, are you able to give me directions, or not?"

"Yes. Yes, I am. Um, let me see. Where's that map of the four corners area?" He rummaged through some papers on a table in the corner and produced a large piece of paper. "Here it is."

He laid the map on his desk and traced the route with his skinny finger.

"How far is this trip?" Mattie hoped it wouldn't take more than six days. Three would be better.

"It's about one hundred and forty miles. I'd say about four and a half days by horseback, but I strongly urge you to give up this notion of riding there yourself. That's pretty barren country out there." He pointed to his window. "It can be pretty rough."

Mattie fought the urge to tell him she'd spent three days on the trail already, before she had to wait for the telegram. She thanked the man and turned to leave.

"Will you be returning to our fair city?"

She shook her head. "Not if I can help it." Mattie didn't look back, but she was certain that cavernous mouth fell open again.

Out on the street, she mused about the last time she'd been in a stagecoach. The thing nearly bounced her brains right out of her skull. After arriving at her destination, she could have started a garden with the amount of dirt and dust on her. No. She would ride. And it would keep Cyrus Braydon from knowing where she was going.

When she returned to her room, Mattie unwrapped the new dress she bought a couple days ago and smoothed out the wrinkles. She opened her carpetbag and frowned. Her clothes looked like a two-year old child stuffed them in. Someone rummaged through her things. She pulled her things out to see if anything was missing. It was all there. The only thing of value she had with her was money and the horse. Having seen her horse in the corral on the way back to the hotel, she knew he wasn't stolen. And she kept her money in a pouch attached to her garter belt.

She looked around the room. Everything else was in order. She refolded her clothes and tucked them inside the bag. Her stomach churned. *Cities.* One more reason why she preferred the solitude of the canyon hideaway. Or was it a hideout? No. She shook her head. Will deserved the benefit of a mother who believed in him.

Putting it out of her mind, she removed her skirt. The stiffness of the pocket reminded her of the note. She read it again. Then she tossed it into the open bag.

Mattie stared at it for a moment. Someone poked through that bag. Would they return? What did they want? Want? Wanted? Will. Someone wanted to know if she found Will. She grabbed up the note and stuffed it into the money pouch. She suspected who that someone was. Cyrus. And he wouldn't get away with it.

Chapter Three

Cyrus knocked on Mattie's door at exactly seven o'clock. She opened it, looking far from the simple woman he first met on the porch of the log cabin. Her hair swirled atop her head, and two ringlets graced her forehead. The dress she wore wasn't fancy, but it looked pretty on her. He liked what he saw. Perhaps if they'd met under different circumstances…

He stopped himself from finishing the thought. "Are you ready for supper, Mrs. Gordon?"

"Yes," she replied, her expression anything but friendly. "I'm hungry. And you might as well call me Mattie."

Cyrus offered her his arm. "All right, Mattie. Please call me Cyrus."

Though Mattie linked her arm through his, she felt stiff and rigid. Cyrus couldn't blame her. After all, he was hunting down her son.

The waitress served their meal in a timely manner. Cyrus shifted in his seat as they both ate the first half of their supper in silence. He couldn't remember the last time he ate a nice meal in the company of a genuine lady. "Mattie. I know this is awkward for you. I've been thinking about you."

"And?"

"I can't help wondering that if we'd met under different circumstances—"

Mattie held up her hand to stop him. "No. Don't say it, please. This has been hard enough for me. I've been thinking about what you said, too, and you're right. There have been clues along the way I should have noticed, but I blinded myself to them."

"You mean you've come to believe it's possible your son could be the man on the wanted poster?"

"Yes." She lowered her gaze to the floor.

"I'm sorry you got caught up in all of this. Why don't you go home and let me handle it?"

"I can't. I have a purpose for finding him. I…I've never prepared him for eternity."

"Eternity?"

"Yes. I need to tell him Jesus Christ loves him. He's waiting to forgive Will of all his sins." Mattie's passion was mirrored in her face. "He wants to wash his heart and make him clean so he can stand before Him on judgment day with a clear conscience."

Cyrus heard all that before from his mother and grandmother. But he'd always believed religion for weak-minded men and women. Yet, when Mattie told it, something drew him to it. Maybe it was the sincerity of her words. They weren't empty sentiments. It was as if she knew something more.

"How about you, Cyrus?" The intensity of her gaze caused his heart to pound furiously in his chest.

"What about me?"

"In your line of work, I'm sure you've given thought about what would happen if you were to get shot and die."

Cyrus shuffled his feet under the table. He never had time to think about eternity. Bringing outlaws to justice kept him busy.

"If you were to die today, would you know where you'd spend eternity?"

"With all due respect, I don't believe all that stuff. Nobody can know anything about life after death." He raised his hand, gesturing for her to stop. "So don't give me any of your preaching. Save it for old men, women and children."

"I'm sorry to hear that, Cyrus. Just because you don't believe it, doesn't mean it's not true. Jesus Christ loves you very much. He knew you before you were formed, and He made a way for us to escape the punishment we all deserve, eternal damnation in hell. His forgiveness is a gift he gives freely to all who ask."

Cyrus stood and shoved his chair under the table. "I need to get to bed. I've got more investigating to do tomorrow."

He did have more work to do, but he hadn't told Mattie the truth. Her words caused his heart to pound inside his chest, and he couldn't understand why this affected him so. He'd heard so many foul and ugly things that they no longer bothered him. So why did these gentle words upset him? He had to get away from them before they seared through his heart.

Mattie stood, pushed her chair back, and faced him squarely. "You mean you're investigating other peoples' private duffel bags?"

"What?"

"You know what I mean." Mattie marched out of the restaurant before him, then turned at the bottom of the stairway to face him, her gentle features a storm of emotion. "I'm talking about the fact that my bag had been rummaged through while I was out."

"Someone rummaged through your things? Are you sure?" Concerned, he took her arm and led her upstairs to her room. She struggled to set her arm free, but he ignored her resistance. At her door, he let go of her and pointed to the lock. "Open it."

"Why? So you can force me to tell you what I know, and nobody will see or hear a thing?"

Cyrus glanced around the hallway. The last thing he wanted was for someone to overhear them. He lowered his voice to a whispered growl. "Mattie, your son's life is at stake here. I think we need to talk. Now we can do this here, where everyone can hear, or we can go inside."

She looked up at him, her eyes narrowed and her mouth tight. Cyrus knew the situation had taken a dangerous turn. He watched her dig her key out of her reticule. She hesitated a moment, then unlocked the door.

He followed her inside, and shut the door behind him, locking it. "Have you seen anyone suspicious hanging around the hotel today?"

She crinkled her forehead. "Only you."

"No, Mattie. I haven't been in your room. Has anything been stolen?"

"No. Nothing. Are you telling me the truth that you haven't been in here at all?"

"Yes, ma'am." He searched the room with his investigative eye. "I don't see anything out of place. Was it real messy?"

"No. Only my bag had been rummaged through."

Another bounty hunter? Could be. But how would they know who Mattie was? Cyrus dogged the Gordon gang for months and didn't even know Will's mother was housekeeping for them until he found the hideout. Another bounty hunter wouldn't know about her.

He walked over to the window and peered out, scanning the street and rooftops for signs that Mattie's room might be watched. Nothing looked out of the ordinary. Then he turned toward her. "This changes everything."

"What do you mean? Why?"

"If you're being followed, you can't go back home now. Not alone." He noticed the concern on her face. "If you know where Will is, you can't go to him either. You might be leading someone right to him."

Mattie placed her hands on her hips. "How convenient. The only way I'm going to be safe is if I go with you, I suppose? And next you'll be telling me I'd better take you to my son to keep someone else from killing him first."

Cyrus gazed toward the ceiling for a moment. "I don't know. I'm going to have to think this through. Do you have any idea what someone was looking for?"

"No. I can't be certain." She looked away as she spoke.

She wasn't telling him everything. That's fine. He always got his man, sometimes with less information than he had now. But this placed him in a whole different situation than he'd been in before. He'd never had to look out for an outlaw's kin.

Someone knew something about Will Gordon, and until he figured this out, Mattie Gordon needed protection. He turned back. She had that female look of insecurity and helplessness that cut through to his tender heart. If only she wasn't so vulnerable, he wouldn't be forced to care for her. Or care about her. He sighed. Women sure do complicate things.

"In the meantime," he said quietly. "Keep your doors and windows locked, and don't go out alone at night." Her facial expression turned grave. "I'll see you in the morning." He stepped into the hallway, closing the door behind him, stopping first to hear the click of Mattie's door lock. Satisfied, he entered his room.

A familiar smell permeated his nostrils. Cigar smoke. He hadn't noticed it in the room when he checked in earlier. Glancing around, he saw the window ajar, the curtains fluttering slightly from the night breeze. The first thing he looked for was his rifle. It remained under the mattress where he placed it. Or was it? He thought he put it farther toward the middle as he always did when he left it in his room, but now it lay close to the edge.

Cyrus investigated the rest of his room. Things were similar to the way Mattie described them when she made her discovery. Everything was there, but moved enough for him to know someone had been there.

Either this hotel had a curious employee, or somebody specifically chose the two of them to spy on. Why? They hadn't ridden into town together, arriving a week apart. Their only common thread was the outlaw, Will Gordon. But who would know that? He needed to ask Mattie more questions in the morning. What led her to Boise City, and who has she spoken to since she got here?

He lay awake long into the night, thinking about Mattie and her son. The three thousand dollars reward would provide what he lacked to buy that little place in Texas. He wanted to get back to his farming roots. Low paying sheriff's jobs weren't going to get his dreams for him. He knew he'd have to make money fast, before he got too old. Dreaming of a new life on the farm suddenly took on a new twist. Being a bachelor all his life, he now found himself wondering what it would be like to take a wife. After all, farming could be lonely without someone to share it with.

If he managed to capture Will Gordon without killing him, maybe his mother would turn softer attentions toward him. He shook his head in the darkness of the night. He didn't even know the woman. Or did he? He knew she was kind, and genuine. She cared for and loved her son, regardless of what he'd done. Not many young men could say that about their mothers.

Cyrus didn't come any closer to solving to his dilemma, and finally fell asleep late in the night.

A knock on his door startled Cyrus awake. He jumped out of bed, grabbed his rifle, and cocked it. He stood in the middle of the room, blinking himself awake, the rifle aimed square at the center of the door. The blinds were pulled on the windows, but tiny bits of daylight peeked out from behind them.

The knocking came again, hard and furious.

"Who is it?"

"It's Mattie. I have to talk to you."

Cyrus grabbed his trousers and pulled them on. He opened the door, and Mattie rushed into the room. "Close the door." Her voice held a command.

"What is it? You look pale."

Mattie held out a piece of paper for him. He took it and looked at it. His eyes opened wide at the hideous sight. It was the wanted poster of Will. His copy. He recognized it by the well-worn folds of the paper and a smear in the upper left corner from where he'd dropped a couple beans on it one time. Over the entire sheet, the words, *don't go to Liberal,* were written in what looked like blood.

Cyrus snatched his waistcoat from where he'd draped it over the back of a chair the night before and searched the inside pocket. The poster wasn't there. He hadn't worn it to supper the night before. The hour he spent with Mattie was the only time anyone could have come into the room.

"What's going on, Cyrus?" Mattie looked as though she were about to cry.

"I don't know." He motioned for her to sit in a chair, and he sat on the edge of the bed. "How did you get this?"

"Someone slipped it under the door after I went to sleep. I found it this morning."

"Why does it say not to go to Liberal?"

"You don't know?"

"No. Do you?"

Mattie stood and paced the room. Her breaths came shallow, and she gulped to get control. Should she trust Cyrus? Could he be lying? Doesn't he know about her meeting Will in Liberal? If not, who does? What would happen to her if she does go? What would happen to Will? *Lord, what should I do?*

Trust him. She knew the author of those words.

But he's a bounty hunter. *He told me he didn't believe in You, Lord.*

I am working in his life. Trust him.

Mattie stopped pacing and stared at Cyrus. He'd cleaned himself up for supper last night and didn't look like a wild killer.

"This is the hardest situation I've ever faced in my life, Cyrus." He nodded his head to her in agreement. "I'm going to have to trust you." She paused, took a deep breath, and continued. "I'm supposed to meet Will in Liberal, Kansas, in one week."

He didn't look surprised. He didn't show any emotion on his face. Had she been wrong about him?

He stood and looked down at her. "Who else have you told this to?"

"Nobody except the man at the telegraph office, but even then it was written in code, so he wouldn't know what it was about."

"I need to talk with him anyway. I'll meet you in the dining room in twenty minutes."

Mattie nodded in agreement. Cyrus opened the door for her and Mattie walked back to her room. When she got there, she lay down on the bed and cried. "Lord, I hope I haven't let you down. I pray I haven't put Will's life in more jeopardy than it's already in. Please protect him. And guide me through this."

She picked up her well-worn Bible. Laying it on her lap, she opened it and read Psalm forty-eight. When she came to the last verse, her heart jumped inside her. *"For this God is our God forever and ever; he will be our guide even unto death."* She knew God would guide her in this time of trouble. But was this a foreshadowing of Will's death? No. It wasn't like Him to bring bad news when she needed guidance and comfort. She was certain this meant that, as long as she had breath, He would be there for her. The scripture brought her comfort and she closed the book and hugged it. *Thank you, Lord.*

There was a knock at her door. "Mattie, it's me." The voice came through the door. She liked the sound of it. Strong. Masculine. Gentle.

Cyrus. Underneath his bounty-hunter exterior, he possessed a tenderness she hadn't seen in a man his age. Usually they've been worn down by time and circumstances. How strange that she would trust the man most likely to kill her son.

Mattie opened the door "I thought we were going to meet downstairs."

He brushed past her. "I got the information I needed and didn't see any need to sit around and wait for ten minutes."

"What did the telegraph operator say?"

"Enough for me to believe he hasn't said anything to anyone about anything that's come across the wires. I wouldn't have thought a man that honest could exist."

Mattie felt sad for Cyrus. His misguided profession kept him in the company of those who lived in the shadows, his world filled with dishonesty and deceit. "Then how else could someone know where I'm supposed to meet Will?"

Cyrus peeked out the curtains. "I don't know. But one thing's for sure. Whoever this is, they know who we both are and that we know each other."

"What are we going to do? There must be others like you out there trying to get my son." Huge tears flooded down her face.

Cyrus stepped up to her and wrapped his arms around her. She buried her face in his shirt and sobbed, unable to stop.

"Shhh. It'll be all right," he crooned, and then kissed her hair. "We'll think of something."

Mattie hadn't been hugged in so many years, she'd forgotten

how wonderful it felt. His arms gave her a sense of security. She enjoyed the feel of his fresh shirt on her skin and the masculine scent she'd long forgotten.

Gaining control of her emotions, she pulled away from him. "Thanks, Cyrus. I'm sorry to be so blubbery."

"Glad to help, ma'am." Mattie watched him go to the window again. "We're going to have to sneak out of town," he told her. "I haven't figured out how yet. Don't know if we're being watched from inside the hotel or out. Maybe both."

Mattie sat on her bed while Cyrus paced the room. She watched him furrow his brows deep in thought. Then he looked up, his dark brown eyes showing the intensity of the man.

"Okay, I've got an idea. You might not like it, but it'll be our only hope to get out of here and get to Will before anyone else does."

Mattie stared at him for a moment. Did he realize what he'd just said to her, a mother whose present purpose was to keep her son alive?

As if he knew what she was thinking, he spoke softly. "Mattie. You have my word. I will do my very best to see no harm comes to your son. He'll get a fair trial, I promise."

"Thank you." She didn't know why, but she felt like she needed to cry again.

Mattie pulled on the clothes Cyrus brought for her. Even living in a log cabin in an isolated canyon, she'd never worn men's pants. Having agreed to his strange plan, she didn't complain. After following Cyrus' instructions about how to make herself look like a man, she took one last look in the mirror before leaving. Pulling her cowboy hat low on her forehead, she knew she could pass for a young man. Amazing. Her heart lightened. Hope arose inside her. The plan might succeed after all.

Cyrus thought of everything. Even getting her a different room under a man's name, George Marks. That way, if someone were downstairs watching her enter the hotel as herself, they'd think she was in for the night. When she comes downstairs disguised as George Marks, carrying his bedroll, Mattie should be able to slip out unnoticed.

Mattie practiced walking like a man, watching herself in the mirror. Remembering Cyrus' long-legged swagger, she tried to imitate it, but ended up laughing herself silly. Finally, she decided on a slower pace. She took a deep breath and left the room.

The plan worked well, as far as she could tell. Walking down the street, no one paid her any attention. She went to the stable where her horse had been corralled this past week and traded him for a black mare.

Now walking into the stable as a man, she took possession of the black, paid the man all outstanding bills, and rode out of town. She prayed no one caught on to her trick. If anyone were waiting for Will's mother to leave Boise City, they would think she was tucked in her room in the hotel, while her horse rested in the corral.

Mattie rode out of town at an easy gait, trying not to attract attention, heading in the opposite direction from Liberal, Kansas. Her heart pounded out in her ears. She had to trust Cyrus. He would be at their appointed meeting place. Fighting the feeling the bounty hunter duped her and was now riding happily toward Kansas, she pressed onward.

Trust him. I am working in his life.

Chapter Four

Mattie rode through the night until every muscle in her body screamed out in pain. She stopped and stretched her limbs. Having missed supper, she ate a slab of beef jerky and a can of cold beans. She'd never been afraid to be alone before, but tonight, every noise sent shivers up her spine. Cyrus left Liberal four hours before her in order to make whoever threatened her think they weren't together.

Would he wait for her as promised? Niggling thoughts played havoc in her mind. Had Cyrus fooled her into riding farther away from Will so he could capture him? She pushed the ideas aside and prayed for God's help and wisdom. Again, she felt His leading to trust the bounty hunter.

Somewhat refreshed, she mounted her horse and rode through the night, keeping the faint glow of Liberal in the distance as she circled the town. Cyrus planned for her to loop back to the other side of town and then ride northeast, keeping the North Star at ten o'clock. Cyrus said he'd find her. Finding people was his profession. Mattie had no reason to believe he wouldn't.

Hours dragged on and Mattie couldn't push herself any further. She had no choice but to stop, wrap herself in her blanket on the ground and sleep a little while.

She awoke to the dim, gray of dawn. Rolling over, she nearly hit someone sitting on the ground beside her. Screaming, she scrambled to stand. Her feet got tangled up in themselves, and she landed on her backside in the dirt.

"It's only me," Cyrus said, an amused smile on his face.

Mattie recovered her breath, then kicked his boot. "How long have you been here?"

"A couple hours."

"Why didn't you wake me sooner?" She stood and packed her bedroll.

"You would have jumped and screamed if I woke you earlier, so what's the difference?"

He was right and it infuriated her. "Any sign of anyone following us?"

"No." He smiled again. "Wouldn't matter. You were sleeping like a log. A coyote howling in your ear wouldn't wake you."

Only four and a half days of this. She hoped she could make it without shooting the man.

After eating a cold breakfast, they packed and rode with haste toward Liberal. The first day on the trail, Cyrus led them in a winding pattern across the flatlands. He explained how every thirty minutes they would get a glimpse of what or who might be behind them, without being discovered. It all seemed covert and mysterious to Mattie. They pushed their horses hard, stopping only to water and rest them. The intensity of their ride kept them silent, until they stopped to make camp that night.

Cyrus wouldn't allow a fire yet, so they sat on their blankets, eating jerky and cold biscuits, drinking water from their canteens, and telling stories from their younger days.

"Why did you become a bounty hunter? You seem like a decent fellow."

"I was a deputy sheriff down in Waco in my twenties. Having grown up on a ranch, I knew how to shoot pretty well. I had a deep respect for the law. To my way of thinking, lawbreakers could live a much better life if they'd follow the rules and stay out of trouble." Cyrus lay on his back, cradling his head on his saddle, and gazed up at the stars. "I wanted to own a spread of my own one day. Maybe get myself a wife, have half a dozen babies, and grow old watching the sunset over the prairie. But on a deputy's salary, I'd be too old to enjoy it by the time I had enough money saved up."

He put his hands behind his head and crossed his ankles. "The sheriff taught me so much, and I was torn between two worlds, the law and ranching. When I watched Sheriff Wilson hand over thousands of dollars to a bounty hunter once, I caught the bug. I could bring outlaws to justice and make a fortune. It's taken me a long time to get the money together, but I've enjoyed the work. Being my own boss, traveling across the west, meeting all sorts of interesting people." He sighed deeply. "It's been a good life."

"What about the wife and babies?"

"Somewhere along the way, I lost sight of that dream." He chuckled, and Mattie liked the smoothness of it. "In all the years I've been doing this, I've never run across a situation like this before. This really beats everything."

"You mean about having the mother of an outlaw accompany you on the chase?"

"Yeah, and actually becoming friends with her and working together. That beats 'em all."

"Who told you we're friends?" Mattie heard him sigh and wished she hadn't been sarcastic with him. So far, he'd proven himself an honest man. "That first night when you stayed at the cabin, I didn't like you."

"I know."

"You were only doing your job. The hardest thing I've ever done in my life was face up to the fact that what you told me was true. My son has been lying to me." Mattie didn't know why she was able to confide in Cyrus so easily. Maybe because it was a dark night and she couldn't see his face. She certainly wasn't developing feelings for him, was she?

"I've never dealt with kin like this. Before, they were just people who thought their families were perfect. Or they lied to cover up the loved one's bad deeds. But you genuinely didn't know about Will. And when you realized the possibility that he's an outlaw, you still loved him. But you want him to face up to his errors. That takes courage." Cyrus rolled onto his side and propped an elbow on the saddle, his head resting in his hand. "I admire you, Mattie."

"I've done nothing more than what God required of me."

"How do you know what God requires of you?"

His question surprised Mattie. It also delighted her. She loved to talk about God. "There are several ways. First, the Bible is filled with God's direction for our lives. It's a guidebook on how to live our lives. If we ask Him for forgiveness for our sins and to come live inside us, He will. We can have a personal relationship with God."

"I've never heard that before. I've always been told God is so big and so far above us mere humans, He doesn't have time to talk to us."

"That's what a lot of people think, but it's not true. He loves us so much He sent us his son to die for our sins. Jesus took our place and pardoned us. He became man to show us the way."

"That sure does make God more accessible to ordinary people. But some sins are too big to be forgiven."

Mattie turned toward him, even though his face remained shadowed by the lack of moonlight. "There is no sin too big for God to forgive."

"Do you really believe that?"

"With all my heart. All you have to do is ask, and your sins will be forgiven. Then the Bible tells us to turn from our wicked ways and sin no more. It is a choice we need to make every day of our lives."

Cyrus rolled onto his back again. "Sure gives a fellow something to think about."

Mattie also lay on her back and stared at the stars for a moment. A question plagued her, but she didn't know if she'd get a truthful answer. "Cyrus?"

"Yeah."

"Have you ever killed anyone?"

Cyrus hesitated. "Nope. I've wounded several while trying to take them in, but I've never killed." He sighed. "Kinda makes me feel good to be able to say that."

"It makes me feel better about you, too." She rolled over and said nothing further, but prayed for Cyrus and Will.

When she awoke six hours later, Cyrus was not there. Neither were the horses. She shot up off the ground and looked around her. Everything was gone, except for a flour sack of food and a canteen. *No! Lord. You told me to trust him.*

Cyrus finished watering the horses and headed back to where he'd left Mattie sleeping. He'd never met a woman who could sleep through so much noise. Deciding to let her sleep, he packed the horses and brought them down to the creek to feed and water them.

His thoughts turned to what she said last night about God. She stated everything so simply, yet there was power behind her words. In a short time, Mattie made more sense than a church full of preachers. He'd been raised to believe in a fearful and unattainable God. Mattie made Him sound real. Did God really love man as much as that?

He heard a woman's cry. His heart leapt into his throat.

Climbing onto his horse, he kicked the horse's flanks. "Haw!" he yelled as he rode up the high banks of the river. At the top of the mesa, he saw Mattie, sitting on her blanket, her head in her hands. He galloped to her and jumped down from his horse. Imagining the worst, he ran over to her. He shouldn't have left her alone. The thought of a rattlesnake bite cut clear through him.

She looked up, her face a storm of emotions. "I thought you left me here."

Cyrus dropped to his knees and gathered her into his arms. How could someone who lived with a gang of outlaws be so vulnerable? "I'm sorry. I didn't think you'd wake up yet." He stroked her dark blond hair. "I may hunt outlaws for a living, but I'm not cruel enough to abandon a woman on the prairie." If she thought him capable of that, then she didn't trust him, and it bothered him. For some reason, he needed her to think of him as a good man.

Cradling her in his arms evoked something inside him. For the first time in his life, he felt the need to protect someone other than himself. He held her while she fought for control of her emotions. Then she pushed away and stood up, a sob escaping from her throat. He caused her this terrible fear. When he found her alone in the cabin, her look was far from frightful. It had been contentment and happiness. Cyrus knew he took those wonderful attributes from her. For the first time in his life, he saw a glimpse of how ruthless and uncaring he'd become. Having pushed others aside in search of evil men for his own gain, he'd forgotten there was still goodness in the world.

Mattie went about her usual privacy time, and grabbed a couple pieces of jerky. Cyrus packed her blanket. He wanted to do more.

Setting out at last, leading them across the prairie, he followed the same pattern as the day before. It looked as if no one pursued them, so in late afternoon he took a straighter path toward Liberal.

Mattie's eyes drooped and dark circles formed under them. Her face looked different from when they met. The week in Boise City refreshed her from her first ride, but now she looked weary. Perhaps it was a combination of her lack of sleep, worry and mistrust of her traveling companion. Cyrus knew Will weighed heavy on her heart, too. They both knew that if things went bad, someone could get hurt, even killed.

Could he devise a plan to take Will prisoner without hurting him? If guilty, Will would make it more difficult for Cyrus. A guilty man fights back hard.

He rode along, lost in his thoughts, Mattie following behind him. A horse's whiney and a sharp scream behind him jolted him. He turned and saw the black horse fall on top of Mattie. Cyrus jumped off his horse and flew to them.

The horse tried to get up off its side, causing Mattie to cry out. Her leg was trapped. Cyrus worked to make the horse lean away from her. Then he dragged her out from under the huge animal.

Mattie sat up and rubbed her leg, wincing. Carefully assessing her ankle, he let out a sigh. "It's not broken, just sprained."

Removing his kerchief from around his neck, he wound it tightly around her already swelling ankle. He retrieved her canteen and gave her a drink. Walking over to the horse, which still lay on the ground, he measured the situation. Seeing a huge gopher size hole nearby, he knew that was how it broke its leg. He retrieved his shotgun, aimed it at the animal's head, and pulled the trigger.

Mattie stifled a cry and Cyrus felt compassion for her. "Might as well camp here for the night," he told her. "We made good progress today."

Cyrus pulled Mattie's things from her horse and carried them about fifty yards away to a dip in the prairie. He spread her blanket on the ground and laid her pack on it to protect it from the wind. Then he went back to where she sat on the ground, slipped one arm under her legs and the other around her waist and lifted her.

"You don't have to carry me. I can walk." She wiped her eyes with her sleeve.

"It's no problem. The more rest you give that ankle, the faster it'll heal." He knew it would heal in its own time, but it felt good to have someone other than himself to look out for. Plus, he enjoyed carrying her.

After setting her on the blanket, he brought his horses up to the camp, and then gathered whatever he could find to make a fire.

"Are you sure we should have a fire?" Mattie asked him, her face showing concern. "What if someone sees it?"

"It'll be all right." She said *we*. Cyrus hadn't been part of a *we* since his sheriffing days. He liked the sound of it.

The sun set beyond the horizon as the fire roared to life. Cyrus fried ham slices and canned beans and made a pot of coffee.

"Mm. Smells good. No one has cooked for me before. I've always been the one to do the cooking."

"And you're a great cook." He remembered the meals he forced her to cook for him at the cabin. His rudeness now offended him. How could he treat a lady like that?

Mattie gave him a sideways smile. "I've only cooked two meals for you."

"Meals fit for a king, as I recall."

"Thank you."

Cyrus nodded. He liked the way they'd become familiar. Like friends. Like Sheriff Wilson and himself. No. Not like that. This was far better than his friendship with the sheriff.

Their supper consumed, Cyrus propped Mattie's sore leg on a full food sack before returning to his own blanket. The last thing he did was lay his rifle in front of him, his hand placed so he could grab it and cock it in one motion.

He certainly hoped he wouldn't need the weapon tonight. Cyrus felt it best not to tell Mattie what he saw after shooting her horse. The poor lady already had a string of bad luck today. No use upsetting her so soon.

Chapter Five

Mattie opened her eyes, and saw Cyrus staring across the plains. "Aren't you going to sleep?" she asked.

"Too much on my mind. How about you?"

"My ankle hurts." She sat up and winced. After settling into a position that didn't cause her more pain, she studied Cyrus closely. Didn't he plan to sleep? He told her building the fire tonight wouldn't be dangerous, yet he looked as if he would pounce on a fly if it got close enough.

"Did I wrap it too tight?"

"No, but it swelled up since I first laid down. I can't get comfortable."

"Since neither of us can sleep, do you feel like riding on?"

"I suppose that's better than just lying here. If I'm going to be miserable, I might as well be miserable on a horse." She remembered her poor animal. Cyrus had too many things to carry, making her wonder if he expected her to ride with him on the same horse.

"You can double up with me," he said as if reading her mind.

Mattie cringed inwardly. She found herself drawn to this bounty hunter in friendship, but the thought of being close to him for a long trip made her uncomfortable.

Cyrus sprang into action. Mattie watched him pack up their belongings and secure them to one horse. She waited while he doused the fire and covered it with plenty of dirt. Then he lifted her, blanket and all, and gently placed her on the back of the horse. He slid into the saddle in front of her and they continued on their way.

Mattie held onto his waist, painfully aware of his closeness. She hadn't been this close to a man in over thirteen years. It felt foreign to her, yet familiar at the same time.

Letting her leg dangle down the side of the horse felt good, and she relaxed.

As the sun rose over the horizon, bright and golden, Cyrus reined his mount by a small stream. "We'll stop here a while to rest and water the horses. Then I'll fix us something to eat."

He dismounted and lifted Mattie down, settling her on her good foot, then he helped her hobble a few yards away and lowered her onto the grassy bank. Carefully unwrapping her ankle, he told her to put it into the water to soak a while. She did as he suggested. The water swirled around her ankle, cool and soothing.

"Thank you, Cyrus. You've been very kind to me."

He nodded. Heading for the packhorse, he rifled through his bundles and returned with an arm wrapped around a couple cans and flour sacks. Mattie groaned. Trail food. How she wished she were back at her cabin, cooking delicious meals for Will and the men. A wave of sadness washed over her. She may never get that chance. Will would most likely go to prison for the rest of his life.

Later, he said, "You aren't hungry?"

She looked down at her plate, still untouched on her lap. "I can't stop thinking about Will. I might never make him another home cooked meal again."

Cyrus reached over and covered her hand with his. "I'm sorry about the pain this is causing you, Mattie."

She studied his masculine face. His look was genuine. This man was an enigma. A kind, caring fellow, and a man hunter all rolled into one. She didn't like the feelings he stirred inside her.

"Is there something bothering you?" she asked.

He picked up a pebble and tossed it into the creek. "I've been wondering who sent you that note on the wanted poster."

"That's a mystery to me."

"Mattie, how did you know Will is in Liberal?"

She sucked in a breath. Dare she tell him about the coded message to Doc Lundine? How much information should she give him? They seemed to be working toward a common goal now to get to Will before someone else in order to keep him from getting killed.

"Your silence tells me you still don't trust me." His tone was quiet, defeated.

"I don't know what to think about you, but I need to trust you. You might be able to understand better than I do what's going on." She took a deep breath. "Will told me if I ever needed him for an emergency to go to Boise City and send a telegram to Doc Lundine in Hays, Kansas. I had to say this in my reply, *Doc Lundine, my boy is very ill and in need of attention. Please advise as soon as possible. Mrs. Gordon.*"

"That's unusual. Then what?"

"I was supposed to wait in Boise City until I heard from Doc Lundine."

"And did you hear from him?"

"Yes. He sent me a telegram. I have it with me, but you'll have to turn around while I get it out."

Cyrus smiled and did as she asked. She dug the message out from her hidden pouch. "Here," she said, handing it over his shoulder. He opened it and read.

"Did you ever leave this in your room?"

"No. It's always been with me."

"Hmm. The only two people who would know about Liberal would be the telegrapher, whom I have eliminated, and Doc Lundine." He handed the telegram back to her.

"Do you suppose the doctor would have a reason to keep us away from Will?"

"It doesn't seem like he would. After all, this system your son set up for you to get a hold of him was for that purpose. He would have no idea why you needed to contact Will."

Mattie read the paper again, although she had it memorized.

"There is one more person who knows about that telegram."

Mattie's head shot up. The realization hit her like a twenty-pound sack of sugar. "Will?"

"Yeah."

"He wouldn't have any need to find the note because he would already know what it said."

Cyrus narrowed his eyes at her. "Maybe it wasn't the note they were after. Have you ever come looking for him before?"

"No. Never." Mattie shifted her legs and winced at the pain in her ankle.

"Are you okay?"

"Yes. It hurts, a lot." Mattie had more important things to think about than her ankle. "If they weren't looking for the telegram, what else could they possibly want?"

Cyrus reached into his waistcoat pocket and pulled out the familiar, folded paper. "This."

"The wanted poster? I don't understand."

"If you've never used the code before, and if your son is indeed guilty, then he would want to make sure it was you who sent the telegram." Cyrus rubbed his chin. "He'd also want to know if anyone put you up to it, if you had a partner."

The pain in Mattie's heart swelled. As each day progressed,

the reality of her son leading a band of outlaws grew. How could she have been so blind to it? She did the best she could in raising him. How could he turn out to be this bad? The evidence weighed heavily against Will. She would be losing him, either to some trigger happy bounty hunter, or to a lifetime in prison. Suddenly feeling much older than her forty-six years, she closed her eyes.

"And when they discovered the poster in my waistcoat, they found out that you knew about the warrants against Will. They probably figured we were working together, and that's why they sent you this warning."

Mattie couldn't finish her breakfast. Her stomach wound into a knot.

"There's something else I've been studying on," Cyrus continued. "Hays is a big cattle town. The trains running through there are a great way to ship beef to the east. This Dr. Lundine may not even be a real doctor. He might be someone your son is using to sell the stolen herds."

She didn't feel like talking anymore. "Haven't we sat here long enough?"

"You're right. Let's hit the trail." He easily swung Mattie onto the horse and pulled himself up.

The long ride gave Mattie time to think and pray. Her life had an up-side down feel to it. The one man she thought to be good may very well be an outlaw, and the other, whom she thought a ruthless man hunter, turned out to be kind and caring. Yet, the good man is hunting her son. It didn't make sense.

Mattie closed her eyes and allowed the warm, summer breeze to blow across her face. Would her life ever be normal again?

Cyrus felt the weight of Mattie's head against his shoulder. Her grip around his waist loosened, and her breathing slowed. He slowed the horse to a walk in order to not disturb her sleep. His heart tugged at his emotions. Besides the obvious, that she was pretty and had a shapely figure for a woman her age, she was sweet, good-natured and caring. The fact that he'd won her trust amazed him. Until Boise City, he wouldn't have thought twice about shooting Will Gordon, if the need presented itself. Now, he would avoid that action at all cost.

He didn't know what they'd find when he got to Liberal, but for Mattie's sake, he'd do his best to take Will in alive. Whether he got the money for this bounty or not, he would quit the business for good. Outlaws getting their dues had been the only consequence to his actions. Until Mattie. Meeting her changed the course of his life. He couldn't remember a single event ever doing that for him.

Truth was, for the first time in his life, he felt needed. Mattie relied on him to save her son from death. In return, he wasn't alone on this trip. Having someone to talk to showed him what he'd been missing. He'd forgotten the softer side of life, and he wanted that. He felt something for Mattie, although he couldn't say what it was. Friendship? Love? No. Couldn't be love.

His thoughts were becoming too deep. Emotions were not something he'd been accustomed to analyzing.

Cyrus forced his mind back to the job at hand. He felt certain Will wouldn't have gone to Boise City himself, but would have sent one of his hired men. If his supposition was correct, they hadn't fooled Will's man. He'd seen evidence of being followed. Was he close enough to watch them this minute? Had he sent Will a telegram when he discovered Mattie gone? Did they pass them in the night? He hoped not. If that were the case, they would be waiting for them. His mind reeled from the myriad of questions.

Maybe Mattie's presence would prevent something terrible from happening. But then again, sometimes outlaws panicked and didn't care who got in their way. Would he be able to protect her, to keep her out of the line of fire should guns come into play? The thought sent a shiver of fear up his spine, ending where Mattie's head rested on his shoulder. He never had to think about it before. It was part of the job. But he wanted to protect Will's mother.

Cyrus worked his lower jaw while he contemplated his next move. The Gordon gang knew he was coming after them. They had to know Mattie accompanied him. He couldn't take a chance with her life.

He turned his horse west. It might mean losing his lead on the gang's present location, but he had something more important to do. He'd take Mattie home to safety.

Mattie woke, and sat up straight. How long had she been asleep? What did Cyrus think of her leaning against him like that?

"How are you doing back there?"

"Uh…" How was she doing? She was embarrassed. "I'm doing fine."

"How's your ankle? Do you need to make a stop?"

"It's throbbing, but stopping won't relieve it much. We might as well keep going. I'm anxious to get to Will."

"Okay." He turned his head to look at her. "But if you need to stop, please tell me."

"I will." *My*. He was using manners now. *What a strange man*. But he was no longer a stranger to her. She felt comfortable with him. They had a common objective, and shared a horse on the long trail to achieve that goal. It felt nice to have someone helping her.

Thank you, Lord. Sending me Cyrus has been a great blessing. I was angry that you'd let my son become what he has. I gave him to You, but when he told me to stop talking about God I didn't want to offend him, so I stopped. It looks like I failed You. Please forgive me. Please don't let Will die before giving his life to You.

She watched the prairie grass go by under the horse's hooves. Wildflowers amongst the weeds. Which was she? The flower or the weed? She felt like a weed right now. Choking out the life of her son. Taking away his freedom, his beauty. She had a knot in the pit of her stomach.

Was she doing the right thing? Finding him and turning him in? What would they uncover when they got to Liberal? If it were one of the boys putting pressure on them back in Boise City, would he tell Will they were coming? Yes. They knew about the bounty hunter. They would be waiting. Ready for him.

Mattie swallowed hard. She didn't want anyone to get hurt, not Will and not Cyrus. She didn't want to witness any of it. She wanted to go home. Try to forget it all. Go back to her sweet life of taking care of her son and the boys.

Cyrus stopped the horses and jumped down. He fiddled with his saddlebags, and fished a piece of paper out of it. Then, as if suddenly realizing she was still there, he looked up at her.

"I have to check the map. Would you like to rest a bit? Looks like another two hours before we make camp for the night."

"Yes. That would be nice."

He helped Mattie down and half carried her to a spot where she could sit on the grass. "Turn around and don't look over here until I say so." Mattie struggled to take care of her personal needs, groaning every time she moved her ankle.

"Are you all right back there?" Cyrus called over his shoulder.

"Yes. Don't look back."

When she finished, she hopped on one leg closer to the horse and let herself down into the grass. She lay on her back in the prairie grass. Only a few wispy clouds floated effortlessly in the light blue sky. She remembered often laying on the ground with Will when he was a boy, each trying to be the first to identify shapes in the clouds. How happy they had been. She made a good life for Will after her husband died.

Cyrus walked over to her, carrying a canteen and a couple pieces of jerky. He handed a piece of beef and the canteen to Mattie. She drank several large gulps of water.

"Thanks. How much longer is it going to take?"

Cyrus sat beside her on the grass and she sat up. He looked everywhere but at her.

"Cyrus, did you hear me?"

"Yes. I heard."

"Is something wrong?"

"No. I'm thinking."

"About what?"

"About how I'm going to tell you what I need to tell you."

Mattie looked at him and frowned. "I've trusted you with the whereabouts of my son. Now it's your turn to trust me."

He took a deep breath and looked down at his hands. "You're right." He nodded and gazed into her eyes in a way nobody had done in a long time. "We've been traveling most of the day away from Liberal."

"What? We're that far off?" Mattie groaned and looked eastward.

"No. It's not that. I decided to take you home."

Mattie snapped her head back toward him. "*You* decided?"

"Listen, Mattie. I was thinking about everything, and it's obvious Will knows I'm coming. That means there'll be gunplay. I didn't want to take the chance—"

"That I'll see you shoot him?" Mattie trusted him, and now he was talking about shooting her boy. Hot tears formed in her eyes and began dropping to her lap. She attempted to get up. Cyrus grabbed her arm to help her. She pushed him away. "Don't. You don't care about me. All you want is your precious three thousand dollars. I should have known better than to trust a bounty hunter."

"You've got it all wrong. What I was going to say is that I didn't want to take the chance of *you* getting hurt."

"Yeah, but someone's going to get hurt. That's your point, isn't it?"

She tried to walk, but fell. Cyrus caught her and held her. He looked intently into her eyes. "Mattie. You have it all wrong. I turned back because you've gotten to me. I care about you, and that means I don't want to see you hurt. That includes the hurt of losing your son. I no longer want to take any chances that either of you might get shot. *Either* of you, Mattie."

Her tears came in torrents now. She believed him. She knew God sent Cyrus to warn her about Will and then to protect them both. He cared about her. After all, this is what she wanted, to go home. Cyrus was giving up his chase. He knew where Will was, and it meant losing a lot of money. He was giving all that up for her.

She grabbed his neck and pulled him toward her. "Thank you," she said into the collar of his shirt.

Mattie didn't know how long they stood on the prairie, intertwined, but it seemed like a fleeting moment before Cyrus broke the embrace. He lifted her off the ground and carried her to the horse.

"We've still got a couple hours to ride tonight. But I suspect we can take it a little easier now."

The next two days plodded along for Mattie. Her back ached, her ankle throbbed, her head hurt. Riding double was harder than single. Not as much room to move around. Her muscles tired quickly from staying in the same position for long periods of time.

Her conversations with Cyrus made it bearable. She discovered many things about him, his childhood, and his dreams for the future. They exchanged tales of their lives and got to know one another better.

There was still one question, but she couldn't bring herself to ask it. Would he resume looking for Will once he left her at the cabin?

When they reached the mouth of the hidden canyon, Mattie smiled to herself. *Home*. She had enough riding to last her the next twenty years. Being gone over three weeks, she couldn't wait to sleep in her own bed again.

The horses started their descent through the rocky crags of the canyon. They rode past the waterfall cascading into a small pond. From there, the water continued in a stream through the floor of the canyon. Mattie thought this was the freshest, cleanest water on the face of the earth.

The walls of the canyon grew taller as they rode deeper into the earth. She enjoyed watching the steep spires appear and disappear in their illusion. High up in the rocks she saw something flash as brightly as the powder from a photographer's trench.

A shot rang out and echoed across the canyon walls. Cyrus tumbled from the horse, dragging Mattie with him. She hit the dirt and crumpled in a heap on the firm ground. She cried out in pain. Glancing over at Cyrus, her heart jumped into her throat. "Cyrus! No!"

Chapter Six

Mattie crawled along the dirt floor of the canyon to where Cyrus lay. Clutching his right shoulder, his breathing was irregular, and he winced in pain. A bright red puddle formed in the dirt beneath him.

Mattie tore off his shirtsleeve and wrapped it around the wound.

"Cyrus," she whispered. He opened his eyes. The pain she saw in them cut to her soul. "I'm sorry. Please hang on. I'll get you to the cabin."

"Are you…were you shot?" His voice came in spurts as shallow as the breaths he took.

"I'm fine. Shh. Don't talk."

Mattie heard horses' hooves approaching and then stop behind her. The sun became blocked by a huge shadow that covered the earth around her. She looked up into her son's handsome face. His rifle lay across the saddle in front of him.

"Step back from him, Mother. He's scum." Will sneered at Cyrus. "He came here to kill me, but the shoe's on the other foot now."

Mattie couldn't believe Will's dangerous look. In that moment, she knew it was true, everything the wanted poster said about him. She fought the urge to cry.

"No. I won't step back." She squared her shoulders. "We didn't know you were here. He was bringing me home because I hurt my ankle."

Will's eyes lowered to her wrapped ankle. "Here, give me your hand and I'll pull you up. You can't walk on that foot."

"Not until I know you aren't going to kill Cyrus."

"Cyrus, is it? When did you become such good friends, Mother?" Will leaned forward and looked closer at the wounded man. "I've heard of you. Big bounty hunter in these parts. Always gets your man. Until now."

Mattie stood, wobbling on one foot. "William Gordon. There'll be no killing on *this* ground. Not as long as I'm here. And I'm not going anywhere for a long time." She narrowed her eyes and felt her jaw tighten. "Now, you tell the boys to bring him up to the cabin. He'll have your room until he's well enough to leave on his own two feet."

"You don't understand, Mother. This changes everything between us."

"It only changes our relationship if you allow it to. The Bible says to love your neighbor as yourself. It hurts me to realize you must not think very much of yourself to be treating others this way." Mattie hopped over to his horse and steadied herself by hugging its neck. "Will, he's not the terrible monster you think he is. How about you? Have you become a monster?"

Mattie watched her son glance around at his men sitting atop of their horses, as if confirming his leadership. Then he looked back at her. "You can play nursemaid if you want to. Just remember, as soon as he's out of this canyon, he's fair game."

"He's a human being, honey. Just like you. And you both deserve to be treated with respect. You are both God's creation, His children."

"Mother, I don't feel like listening to your preaching today." Will gave a shrill whistle and two of his men rode up beside him. "Take him to the cabin."

The men swung down from their horses and sauntered over to Cyrus. One of them grabbed hold of his shirt and yanked him to his feet. Cyrus let out a cry of pain.

Mattie hobbled over to them and whacked Bob on his back. "You treat him gentle." Bob blinked at her like a frog in a hailstorm. He glanced toward Will.

Will nodded, and the men picked Cyrus up gently and led him to a horse. They hoisted him up, and Bob rode behind him. Mattie traveled with Will the rest of the way through the canyon to the cabin.

When they got Cyrus into bed, Mattie began nursing his wound. The bullet went clear through his shoulder, and it looked like he would heal. She sat with him until he fell asleep, then crept out of the room.

Will sat in the rocker by the fireplace, smoking a pipe. "Is he going to live?"

"Yes, I think so."

"Too bad."

His lack of concern hurt Mattie. She pulled up a chair and sat across from him. "What happened to you? How long have you been rustling cattle and horses?"

He shrugged his shoulders. "I guess it don't hurt to tell you now. Been at it for about ten years."

"Ten years. Why you'd have only been fifteen. How did you get started?"

"Remember Mr. Simms? I worked for him that summer on his ranch. I loved ranching. But old man Simms didn't let me do the things he let the boys with fathers do. He said it would be too dangerous for me. I had a mother to take care of. He said if I were to fall and break my neck, there'd be nobody to watch out for you."

"I'm sorry, honey. I had no idea how much pressure you were under. Did Mr. Simms make you rustle cattle?"

"No. It was another fella who came to work there in July. After he saw I was willing and capable of handling myself, he offered me a job. Said it might be dangerous, but we wouldn't tell you. So, I quit working at the Simms place and went to work for Manney." He rocked back and forth, his head held high. "Been rustling ever since."

"I've been cooking and cleaning up for a gang of outlaws all this time." Mattie stared into the empty fireplace. It mirrored how she felt at that moment. No fire left to warm her heart.

"If it's any consolation, the men all love you. They wouldn't do anything to hurt you. You were more mother to most of them than their own."

"How about you, Will? How do you feel about me?"

"You're all right. Never been too pushy or nosey. Treated me well."

She waited for him to tell her he loved her, but the words never came. She hung her head and went to her room, stopping in the doorway. "Good night, son. Thanks for not killing Cyrus."

"Are you sweet on him?"

"Honey, you know me by now. I care what happens to everyone."

"You didn't answer my question."

"I don't know the answer." She entered the room and heard Will's voice through the closed door.

"If that don't beat all. My mother's sweet on the bounty hunter who came to kill me."

She got ready for bed, pulled back the sheets, and lay on top of them. Yes. She was sweet on Cyrus. True, he was a bounty hunter. But he was a decent and kind man. Until he came along and put a gun to her head, she hadn't really experienced much of anything. She'd been content to live her days cooking and cleaning after everyone. But was she really happy?

Whenever Will was gone, she enjoyed not having ten men to look after. But if she were honest with herself, she was lonely. Lonely for someone her own age. A friend she could talk to and share a life with. She never voiced her desire for a mate in her prayers, but it had always been there in the back of her mind.

Maybe she even loved him. Was it possible after only three weeks? In her prayers, she thanked God for bringing Cyrus into her well-ordered life. He shook things up around here. She liked that. *Lord, please don't let me nurse Cyrus back to health, only to have Will shoot him dead.*

Mattie had no chance to stay in bed and prop her foot up on a pillow the next morning. The men were back and needed her to look after them. She looked in on Cyrus first. He still slept, so she crept out.

She limped around the kitchen, cooking breakfast for a gang of outlaws. That was how she regarded them now. They would never again be 'her boys.' The food prepared, she went outside to the porch and rang the chow bell.

Cowboys poured from the bunkhouse, Will and Bob from the barn. They noisily sat themselves at the table and gobbled up the food as fast as Mattie could set it in front of them.

"We sure did miss you, Mother Gordon," Bob told her. "Ain't nobody who can cook as good as you."

The men grunted their agreement and Mattie thanked them. Twenty minutes later, they began filing out of the cabin to go about whatever they needed to do that day.

She took a bowl of broth and a couple biscuits to Cyrus. When she felt his forehead for fever, he opened his eyes. "It's about time you woke up." Mattie smiled at him. "Your fever is down."

"Where am I?"

"You're in Will's room. You were shot yesterday. Do you remember?"

He closed his eyes and winced. "Yeah, I remember," he said weakly. "It took guts to stand up to him like you did. You're quite a little lady."

"Hush up and eat this." Mattie spooned some broth into his mouth and then gave him a bite of the biscuit. He ate everything she gave him, then closed his eyes and went to sleep.

Mattie cleaned the breakfast dishes, then headed to the river to get another bucket of water. Activity buzzed all around her in the yard. Three men stood on the corral fence, looking over a new horse. Will chopped firewood beside the house. Four cowboys sat around a table outside the bunkhouse, playing cards. Bob was looking over her chickens. Nine men accounted for. Maggie was certain Jake would be hiding in the rocks a quarter of a mile from there, gun ready to shoot anyone who might invade their hideout. She cringed at the thought. All those years, and she never questioned why they needed a man to keep an eye on the entrance to the canyon.

She threw the bucket into the river and pulled it back to shore with the rope attached to the handle. Bob appeared behind her. "I'll carry that for you, Mother Gordon."

"Thanks Bob, but I can do it myself." He smiled and grabbed the bucket from her anyway.

"Here, lean on me." She was grateful for the help. Her ankle throbbed. "I was wondering something, Mother Gordon. If I was to catch you two or three of them chickens, do you think you could roast 'em up for supper tonight?"

Mattie always liked Bob. Sometimes he treated her kinder than her own son did. Like now. When she hobbled past Will, leaning on the tall cowboy for support, he looked up with no particular expression. But Bob was more gentlemanly and often helped her with her chores.

"Will you clean the chickens for me, Bob?"

She didn't know how, but his smile became brighter. "Sure thing, Mother Gordon."

"All right. You catch 'em and I'll cook 'em."

"Whoopee! We're gonna have ourselves a feast tonight."

Bob set the water bucket on the Hoosier cabinet. "Anything else I can do for you before I go?"

Mattie thought for a moment, then pulled up a chair and sat. She motioned for Bob to sit across from her, and he did. In a voice near a whisper, she asked him the question burning in her heart. "Did Will really kill a man?"

Bob's smile instantly disappeared. His eyes darted to the door. Thinking someone might be there, she turned to look, but it was still closed. She wondered what he was frightened of.

He leaned over the table and looked her in the eyes. "Mother Gordon, there's some things best left alone."

"You mean you don't know, or you won't tell me?"

"A little of both, ma'am."

"What do you know?"

Again he looked toward the door. He leaned forward and lowered his voice. "Will had this gal down in Texas. She was married, but that didn't make any difference to either of them. She was Will's age, but her husband was older. He was on the town council and owned several businesses in town, a right respectable man."

Mattie's stomach churned. Maybe she really didn't want to hear this.

"I guess they got caught kissing. The rest I only know from what people have told me."

"What do they say happened?"

He leaned even closer. "The way Will tells it, the man took a hand gun out of his waistcoat pocket. He aimed, and Will jumped out of the way. The lady screamed and lept into the line of fire. She was hit. Killed instantly."

Mattie felt faint. She closed her eyes, her head reeling. But she needed to know. "Go on." Her words were barely a whisper.

"The man was shocked at what he'd done, he ran to his wife and Will got away. The next thing we know, there's a wanted poster out on Will for murder."

The cabin door opened and they both looked up. Will stood in the doorway, frowning. "Go about your business, Bob."

Bob didn't say anything, but stood and rushed out the door. Her son was younger than Bob by about eight years, yet he held some sort of power over him.

"You want to ask questions, Mother, you ask me." He left the cabin, slamming the door behind him.

Mattie laid her head down on the table and cried for her son. How had he been able to keep this outlaw life a secret from her? A wildflower amidst the weeds. He wasn't the beautiful flower she once thought him to be. He was a weed, one of the ugliest and deadliest. Whether he killed that girl or not, she was dead because of him and his lustful sin. How could she bear this plight?

She checked on Cyrus. He was sleeping. She limped to her own room and locked the door behind her. Throwing herself on the bed, she sobbed into her pillow.

When the tears would flow no more, Mattie rolled over onto her back, propped her foot up with a pillow and prayed. She prayed for her son, Cyrus, Bob and the rest of the gang. She prayed for herself and for wisdom and guidance. She opened her Bible and began to read where she left off the previous night. Psalm eighteen. It addressed her present needs, comforting her.

'In my distress I called upon the Lord, and cried unto my God; He heard my voice out of his temple and my cry came before him, even into his ears.'

She closed the worn, old book and shut her eyes. God heard her cry. He was still in control.

Mattie left her room with her heart renewed, trusting God to work everything out for everyone's good. She fixed lunch for the men and again, they ate like hungry pigs, leaving her alone to clean up.

She woke Cyrus and fed him his bland lunch of chicken broth and biscuits, and he fell asleep while Mattie read to him from the Bible.

Mattie was glad he allowed her to read the Bible to him. She chose parts that were particularly important to forgiveness from his sins. A couple times, he asked her to explain what it meant and she did the best she could.

He would shake his head in frustration. "There's got to be more to it than that."

Mattie assured him God's forgiveness was simple and for everyone. She began finishing their time together by praying for him. In her heart, she felt assured that it wouldn't be much longer before he would accept the gospel message.

She kept praying for her son, too, and tried to talk about God with him, but he would have nothing to do with it.

Cyrus grew stronger and after only a couple days, was able to sit up and walk to the kitchen table and back to his bed. Mattie enjoyed having someone her own age to talk to and laugh with.

One day, as Cyrus walked around the kitchen, strengthening his muscles, Will entered the cabin.

"Well, well. What have we here?"

"Leave him alone, Will," Mattie told her son. Until that time, she'd managed to keep the two apart.

"You about ready to leave? Huh, Mr. Bounty Hunter?" Will shoved a finger into Cyrus' chest.

"Will. That's enough." Mattie wedged herself between them.

"I wonder what you'll do when you get out of here? Go settle down in a little place on the edge of a town? Maybe have a white picket fence around the yard? Raise some young'uns?"

Cyrus smiled at him. "Actually, that doesn't sound too bad. Except I'd rather have a farm."

"Is that a fact? Bounty hunter turned farmer. Did you ever hear of the likes of that before?" Will laughed and pushed Mattie aside.

"Will, he's not doing anything to you. Leave him alone."

"Mother, stay out of it. It's between him and me." Will pulled his handgun out of its holster and began waving it in front of Cyrus' face. "I told him I'd let him leave when he gets better. I never guaranteed how far he'd get."

Lord, what can I do? Will is so angry.

A thought came to her, and she knew God answered her hasty prayer. "You're both going to have to get out of my kitchen now if I'm going to get that chocolate custard pie made for supper."

"Chocolate custard pie?" Will smiled. "We haven't had that in a long time." He replaced the gun in the holster and walked toward the door. Before he exited, he turned back toward Cyrus. "Don't think about trying to leave. My man won't miss next time."

Cyrus plopped into a chair. "I can't leave, and I can't stay. This is the first time in my life the outlaw has the upper hand."

Mattie sat in a chair across from him. "And I'm afraid it's all my fault."

He reached over the table and took her hand. "How do you figure that?"

"If I hadn't followed after you in the first place—"

"I wouldn't be sitting here admiring your beautiful blue eyes."

His sweetness in the face of danger brought tears to her eyes, but she held them back.

"You told me God had a plan for everyone's life. It would be easy to believe if you're part of that plan for me."

"But Cyrus—"

He grinned playfully at her. "You'd better hush up and get some chocolate custard pies made, or we'll both be in trouble tonight."

His dark brown eyes looked worn and tired, so Mattie sent

him to bed to rest. She made the pies, and the men lauded her when she produced them after supper. Will ate two pieces and smiled at her before he left the house for the night. The first one he'd given her since they'd returned home.

The next day Bob helped Mattie carry the wash down to the stream. Years prior, Will strung up a line right beside the water for her to hang the clothes. When Bob set the basket down, he looked as though he wanted to say something.

He bent down, picked up a shirt from the top of the pile and handed it to her. "I've got something to tell you, and you need to not show any reaction." Bob whispered through his teeth, barely moving his lips.

Her heart fluttered a moment. She took the shirt from him, grabbed a cake of soap and headed for the water's edge. Plunging and scrubbing, she waited for what he would say next.

"Will's looking for a way to knock off Mr. Braydon. No matter what happens, that man's not going to leave here alive. I thought you should know."

She finished the shirt and turned to hang it. Bob was gone.

Mattie fought the panic threatening to overtake her. Her worst suspicious were confirmed. How could she get Cyrus out of the canyon? The rest of the morning she scrubbed clothes and petitioned God on behalf of Cyrus.

When she went inside to fix the men's lunches, she told Cyrus what Bob told her. Cyrus' expression didn't change. He must have known all along he wouldn't be walking out of there.

"I guess you'll just have to pray harder," he said.

Mattie hit him on his good arm. "It wouldn't hurt you to do some praying of your own."

"Desperate times make men do desperate things."

"Oh, Cyrus. Don't make fun of my faith. And don't pray only out of desperation. Pray because you want to."

He touched her cheek, sending shivers down her spine. "How long has it been since a man has kissed you?"

Mattie's jaw loosened. She thought it might come unhinged. He wanted to kiss her. She ached for it to happen. Until this moment she hadn't realized how much she was attracted to him.

"No. You dare not. What if Will came in?"

"Then I go out of this life with a smile on my face."

Mattie hit him in the arm again. "Don't even joke about it. I've got to fix lunch, while you go into that room and think of a way to get out of here."

"Yes, ma'am." He left her alone.

Mattie's heart wouldn't stop fluttering. She thought of his offer to kiss her. Not for the world had she ever thought a kiss could lead to death. If kissing him would keep him alive, she'd do it without regret. She gazed out the window, the bread she started to cut all but forgotten on the table. What would it have been like to be kissed by Cyrus? Would he have been tender, or playful? She imagined his lips against hers.

She shook her head and resumed slicing the bread. No use thinking about it. It would never happen if they didn't think of a way for Cyrus to escape this prison. And it better be soon.

Chapter Seven

Cyrus remained a prisoner in the cabin.

Due to Will's contempt of him, he didn't venture out of the bedroom whenever Will and his men were in the house. After the men finished their meals and left, he sneaked out and talked with Mattie, but it made her nervous; he wouldn't stay in the front room for long. He'd already looked for an escape route by surveying the terrain through all the windows in the cabin. It wouldn't work. They kept a guard in the rocks and another walking around the compound.

Cyrus sat on the bed, staring through the window at the world outside, feeling like a trapped animal. He now understood the life he sentenced many men to. He also knew he could never enjoy being a bounty hunter again. The money was good, but at what price? It cost him his freedom, a normal life, and his compassion for others. It took meeting the mother of one of the most wanted outlaws in the west, and being held prisoner, to realize what his chosen path had cost him.

No one on the outside would know if he didn't get out of this canyon alive. No one would care. He would pass out of existence and not a soul would come looking for him. The thought saddened him.

Mattie would be the only person who might mourn him. Their stolen talks brought them together as allies during his confinement. He longed to hold her close like he did on the trail, and he wanted to kiss her. But that was too dangerous. If Will caught him with his mother, there'd be no telling what the man might do. After all, he was wanted for murder. Mattie could get hurt. The thought of her being harmed because of him was too much for him to bear. He'd never had someone to love and protect before.

Love?

Cyrus sat on the edge of the bed and admitted to himself, he loved Mattie. The only way he could protect her was to escape and leave her there.

Lord, if you're real like Mattie says, then I ask you to protect her. Please don't let anything happen to her on my account. The prayer came surprisingly easy to him. His grandmother made sure he said his prayers each evening when he was young. The feeling that he was no longer alone in the room overwhelmed him.

I know You are real, but I wanted to live my own way. I didn't want anyone else to 'direct my path' like Grandma always said. But I've made a mess of it. I've put myself and Mattie in jeopardy. I've lost contact with the real world. I've tracked down and hunted men like the Indians hunt buffalo.

Discovering how he'd given no regard to human life sickened him. It never mattered to him whether the hunted was guilty or innocent. All he was after was money. Greed had motivated him.

Please, God, forgive me for my mistakes and my sins. I don't want to turn my back on You any longer. The life I mapped out for myself holds nothing for me.

Warmth covered Cyrus like a blanket. Tears formed in his

eyes and slid down his cheeks. He wiped them on his shirtsleeve. He felt forgiven. God was giving him another chance to live his life right. His heart beat a steady rhythm. For the first time in his life, he felt truly clean.

"Thank you," he whispered. He sat in the quiet room, at peace with himself and the world. It was a feeling to which he could put no name. Cyrus remained still for some time before his thoughts began to wander back to his present situation. They came at him like bullets shot out of a rifle. He wanted to quit bounty hunting and start a new life. Needed to escape. Buy a farm. Take a wife. Mattie.

Lord, my feelings for Mattie are strong. I'm putting us both in danger by staying here. I'm afraid I might do something to bring down her son's anger on her. Please help me to get out of here. I'll figure out how to get Mattie away from Will once I know we are both safe. Please help me.

He stood and walked to the window, staring out at the huge canyon wall looming in front of him across the river. The river, only twenty-five feet away, was free to pass through the canyon. Probably on its way to Mexico.

The river was free to leave the canyon. The thought echoed through his mind. He studied it closer. From their ride into the canyon, he knew it was deep and swift. There were spots where it ran more slowly than others, like the place where he watched Mattie draw water and wash clothes.

Did they have a canoe or boat? No. That wouldn't work. There wouldn't be a way he could get to it without someone seeing him.

He observed a large piece of driftwood floating by. Looking from the scrub pines to the river, and then to the walls of the canyon itself, a plan formulated in his mind. If it worked, he would be free by morning.

* * *

Cyrus devoured his breakfast while Mattie cleaned up the dishes from the other men. "Mattie," he said between bites. "How far does the river flow before it leaves this canyon?"

"Oh, I'm not too sure. The canyon narrows about a fourth of a mile from here. The only thing that can get through it is the river. There's no place for man or beast to get through on foot."

"That's why Will doesn't have a guard posted on that end of the canyon." He finished his bacon and gulped down the rest of his coffee.

"Exactly." Mattie stood at the end of the table, wiping her hands in a towel, eyeing him curiously. She looked like she wanted to say something, but didn't. The less she knew, the better it would go for her.

"Cyrus." She lowered her voice and spoke with urgency. "Please don't do anything to get hurt."

"Don't worry. I got someone with me now who wants to take care of me." She gave him a puzzled look, and he smiled. "A while ago, I asked God to forgive me of my sins and guide my life. And He did it, Mattie."

She threw her arms around his neck and hugged him. "Praise God." She'd forgotten to keep her voice down, and her excitement reciprocated inside him. Then she drew away, her gaze darting toward the door fearfully, the feel of her arms around him still fresh against his neck. "This is such an answer to prayer, Cyrus," she said quietly. "You have no idea how happy this makes me."

"That makes two of us."

She went back to doing the dishes, but now began humming a soft hymn. Cyrus didn't know the words, but it had a familiar ring to it. Her reaction moments ago cemented his plans firmly in his mind. He could never put Mattie in danger. He'd have to leave.

His mind worked through his plan. He'd probably have to

abandon his horses there at the hideout. He hated to lose them. They'd been faithful to him. Once outside the canyon, he could implement some of the Indian tricks he'd picked up on how to hide out on the prairie. Springfield was the nearest town, but it was possible the Gordons had friends there. How else could they have remained hidden all these years? No, he'd have to head south. It would take him four or five days to make it to Boise City on foot. He'd have to carry enough rations to last that long.

He dwelled on his plan through the day. There was only one thing missing. The actual getaway. It amazed him that after praying about it, he felt at peace. He had no anxiety over it. Somehow, he knew that God was working on his behalf, and the thought brought tears to his eyes.

Cyrus sat on the bed, eating the last of Mattie's delicious stew and biscuits. He listened to the men talking, their voices muffled through the walls of the cabin. A poker game was planned, and those not participating were going to sit on the bunkhouse porch, enjoying the stars. One of them agreed to play his harmonica. Cyrus bristled at how normal it all sounded. How could lawbreakers go about their lives as if they had no cares in the world? No wonder Mattie hadn't caught on to their ruse.

Then, he heard the sound of chairs scraping across the floor and the scuffling of boots clunking out the door. Bob's voice was the only one he heard who took the time to thank Mattie for her meal. He was a nice man, for an outlaw.

He lay back on the bed and read the Bible. And he waited.

The familiar tapping at his door brought a smile to his face. "Come in."

Mattie entered the bedroom and picked up the tray with his empty dishes.

"Thank you for that wonderful meal. You are the best cook I've ever met."

She grinned. "I'm probably the only cook you've actually met."

He wanted to grab her and kiss her. Couldn't he sneak her out with him? He knew the answer, and it brought a pain to his heart. It would be dangerous enough for himself. He wouldn't take the chance of Mattie getting hurt.

She headed for the door, but turned and looked at him. Her face held a mixture of emotions, as if she somehow knew this might be their last meeting. But he knew she would be careful. "Goodnight."

"Goodnight."

"May God go with you."

Cyrus didn't know how to respond. God would be his only hope. He heard Mattie's delicate footsteps in the big front room, and then the door to her room beside him closed.

He turned out his lamp and waited.

Being at the back of the house, Cyrus could only guess the men had finished the game and retired for the evening by the way the sky darkened suddenly. They must have put their lights out. He knew there would be two guards, one in the rocks a quarter of a mile upriver, and the other one wandering around the yard. That was the one he had to worry about most.

Still he waited.

He wanted to go, but something within him held him in his bed.

After another hour, he sneaked into the kitchen and stashed food into a flour sack. It had to be food that wouldn't be ruined from being in the water; apples, oranges, jerky, carrots, beets. He returned to his room and rummaged through Will's drawers. Finding a pair of jeans, he stuck a belt through the loops, pulling as hard as he could. He stuffed the food into the waist of the pants before pulling them almost completely closed. He brought the bottoms of the legs around his middle, and tied them into a knot. The seat of the jeans hung behind him like a huge extra pocket. Then he sat back down and waited, but he didn't know how long he'd need to stay in the room.

Then he heard it. A scream rang out in the night, like a baby wailing. The hairs on the back of his head stood up on end. What was that? The screaming came closer, and then he heard the chickens squawk loudly. Something was trying to get at them.

A growl like a big cat mixed with the din from the chickens. *A bobcat.* The yard became a mixture of noises as the men awoke and began hollering orders to one another.

Cyrus knew he would never get another chance like this one. He sneaked out of the room and across the darkened front room. When he slowly peeked out the front door, Mattie's back was to him as she stood at the end of the porch, watching the scene in the yard. Shots rang out, the cat growled again.

Cyrus ran off the other end of the porch, so Mattie wouldn't see him. He circled the cabin and leaned up against the clapboard walls. Men were running toward the chicken coop, shouting and shooting wildly. *Lord, please help me.*

He ran toward the river, stopping to pull a small scrub tree out of the ground. Then he plunged into the frigid water, hiding his head behind the branches. The river carried him away from the noise, and no one even noticed. He prayed they wouldn't check his room until morning.

Cyrus floated through the darkness and around a bend. The noise became muted until he heard nothing at all but the river hurrying over the rocks. The water swirled around him as he floated along, its icy wetness causing him to shiver. Even through the dark, he could discern the huge, sheer cliffs of the canyon towering high above him. Dark, foreboding masses of sheer rock. He must have made it to the place where only the river could pass through.

He drifted for what seemed like another half an hour before

the rock cliffs grew shorter. It must be the end of the canyon. Then he heard the rushing of water and knew it was time to go ashore. Kicking his feet, he pushed the branch to his right. His limbs were numb, and he didn't make progress toward the bank very fast. When he finally pulled himself onto dry ground before reaching the rapids, Cyrus had spent his energy. He shivered violently, teeth chattering.

Needing to push on, he picked himself up and forced his legs to move forward. Using the stars and moon to guide him, he stumbled toward Oklahoma.

Mattie, having overslept due to the bobcat ruckus the night before, served the men their breakfast and waited until they left the house to take a tray to Cyrus. She knocked, but didn't hear a response. He must have overslept too. She opened the door and peeked inside. The room was empty.

Her head reeled, and she nearly fainted. Where was Cyrus? He hinted of possibly escaping last night, but she didn't think he would actually do it. Had he made it out of the canyon? Will hadn't said anything about it at breakfast. Nor had any of the other men. She shut the door and returned to the kitchen.

Please, Lord. Help him get far away from here. Protect him from animals and men. And don't let Will notice Cyrus is gone for a while yet. I ask this in Jesus' name, Amen.

Mattie quickly cleaned off Cyrus' plate. If anyone saw it full of food, they would become suspicious. She finished the dishes, took up the water bucket, and went to the river. Casually she looked toward the corral. Both of Cyrus' horses were still there. How had he been able to leave without them? Then she remembered him asking about the river's course. While filling the bucket, she ventured a look down river. Had he really jumped into the water? When? She smiled when she realized the bobcat would have been a perfect diversion.

Thank you, Lord. I know You are with him.

She returned to her work with a lighter heart. Will would probably accuse her of helping him get away. She raised her head. Mattie didn't fear her son or the boys. Especially the boys. They'd keep Will from harming her.

He got away. The words resounded in her ears throughout the rest of the day. The men never checked on Cyrus that day, nor the next. Mattie was amazed. Until his escape, she'd been emptying his chamber pot for him. To keep Will from becoming suspicious, every now and then throughout the day, she put water into the pot and poured it outside. Let the men think what they wanted to.

The next day came and went and Cyrus was not discovered missing. Mattie thanked God for giving him this head start. Two full days. He could be as many as forty miles from there by then, maybe more.

The third morning after Cyrus left, Will hung around after breakfast to talk to Mattie. "How's the bounty hunter been treating you? Sweet as honey?" The words were said with a sneer on his face and contempt in his voice.

Mattie's heart stopped a moment. She turned from him to work on the dishes so she wouldn't give anything away.

"He's been no trouble."

"And it's about time I make sure he never gives anyone any trouble ever again."

Mattie flung around. "What do you mean?"

Will headed toward his room. "I think you understand me, Mother."

Mattie stood between him and the door. "I can't let you do this, Will. Consider your soul. Please don't let your heart become so hard that you would resort to killing a man in cold blood."

Will stared at her a moment.

"What kind of monster have you become, Will Gordon? If

you're truly not guilty of this murder you're wanted for, then why not go back to Texas to clear your name?"

"I'd never get a fair trial." He took hold of her shoulders and stared into her eyes. "There were no other witnesses. The man is respected in town. Everyone believed him. I have no proof that I didn't kill Sarah."

"There's got to be someone who could help you."

"There's no one, Mother!" he shouted, his hot breath only inches away from her face. "Don't you understand? The law is corrupt. It doesn't work the way it's supposed to. And men like Braydon are part of the problem. I won't let him take me in."

He pushed her aside and kicked open the door. "Bounty hunter!"

Mattie held her breath.

"What? Where is he?"

"I don't know. Isn't he in there?"

"No. He's out." Will ran past her and out the door.

She followed him onto the porch. Will shouted orders to each man to saddle their horses. He barked for them to scatter to look for Cyrus. The men scrambled at his command.

Within minutes the camp cleared out, leaving Mattie alone. Not quite alone. She suspected the guard would still be at the entrance to the canyon. She knelt right there on the porch and prayed fervently.

The men returned to camp that evening. Mattie watched Will kick and stomp and huff around the yard as each man reported to him. He entered the house and grabbed Mattie by the arm, twisting her around to face him.

"What do you know about this? Where is he? How did he get past the guard?"

"I don't know."

He shook her with both hands. "Tell me where he is."

The click of a gun hammer sounded from the doorway. Warm tears stung Mattie's eyes, but she recognized Bob through the blur.

"You leave her alone, Will," Bob growled.

Will dropped Mattie's arms and walked over to his man. He grabbed the pistol out of his hand and hit him in the chin. "That's why I'm the boss and you're not," he seethed. "Now get up and get the men packing. We can't stay here any longer."

He glared at Mattie. "Pack everything you can in bundles and be ready to leave within the hour. We won't be coming back here. Thanks to your friend, every lawman in the country will know where this place is by the end of the week."

Will stormed out of the cabin. Mattie rushed to Bob. "Are you all right?"

"Yeah. I'll be okay. You'd better do what he says. You'll be fine, Mother Gordon. None of us men will let any harm come to you."

"Thank you, Bob. Unfortunately, there is one man whom I've come to fear." She sobbed openly, and Bob pulled her to his shoulder.

Within an hour, the whole camp was ready to leave. They formed a train of horses and began the trek out of the canyon. Mattie's tears had hardly stopped since the scene in the kitchen with Will. She loved this place. It held many happy memories for her. But those memories had been false. Will had been lying to her for years.

We won't be coming back here.

Her son's words rang in her head. How would Cyrus ever find her? Would he want to? Her heart cried out to him. Cyrus, please come find me. I love you.

Chapter Eight

Cyrus awoke and looked around. He lay in his long-handle underwear on a soft bed in an airy room. Where was he? Attempting to sit up, every muscle cried out in protest. He flopped back on the mattress and moaned. How did he get here?

Waiting a few moments before trying again, he forced himself to sit up and dangle his legs over the side of the bed. In a flood of emotions, everything came back to him. He remembered the long days walking out on the prairie. His food had given out, and he didn't have any water for what seemed like a couple days. Had he blacked out?

Cyrus glanced around the room for his clothes, but they were gone. Someone knocked on the door, and he covered himself with the blanket. A young lady entered, carrying a tray of delicious smelling food.

"*Señor,* you must get back into bed. You are in no condition to be up." The black haired beauty put the tray onto the table and helped him lie against the pillows as if he were a child.

"Where am I?"

"You are in the Black Mesa. My brother found you and went to town to get a doctor for you. Doc said you suffer from dehydration and overexertion."

"I need to talk to a sheriff."

"You eat first."

"Miss, would you bring the sheriff to me while I eat?"

"Si, señor." Her smile was pretty, and her dark eyes glistened. "I'll be back soon. I don't know how soon we can get the sheriff here."

"Thanks. I appreciate it. What's your name?"

"I am Theresa Montoya."

"Señiorita Montoya, I am Cyrus Braydon."

"Señor Braydon." Theresa worked her tongue to pronounce his name exactly as he had. She nodded when satisfied with her pronunciation and left the room.

Cyrus sat up and gobbled his food.

The young lady returned as he finished the last of his eggs. *"Señor,* my brother sent for Sheriff Tolaine."

"Thank you, miss."

She took the tray away, and Cyrus lay back on the bed and fell asleep. He awoke when he heard a knock on the door. The young *señorita* entered, followed by another man.

"Señor, the sheriff is here." She left the men alone.

Cyrus related everything about the Gordon gang while the sheriff listened with interest.

"We'll form a posse right away. How soon do you think you'll be able to ride? I don't think I could find the entrance to that hidden canyon without you. I never even heard of it before this."

Cyrus sighed. He knew he needed rest, but what ailed him wasn't anything life threatening. "I'll be ready as soon as I locate my clothes. And I'll need a horse. I had to leave mine behind."

"Done." The sheriff shook hands with Cyrus. "We'll meet you at the livery."

Cyrus nodded. "Could you do me a favor and ask the *señorita* where my clothes are? Oh, and I'll need a gun, too."

The sheriff nodded and left the room. Ten minutes later the young girl knocked on his door and entered carrying his clothes, which looked freshly washed and folded.

"Gracias," he said, using one of the very few Mexican words he knew.

The girl beamed at him. "You got a girl, no?"

"Si, señorita. I got a girl." Cyrus prayed Mattie was all right. When Will discovered him missing, did he pour out his anger on her?

She pouted, then shrugged her shoulders.

"Where are the things I had in my pocket?"

Theresa pointed to a bureau across the room. Relieved when he saw his money, he asked her to retrieve it for him. Amazing how Will and his gang only took his rifle and Bowie knife, but left his cash alone. Perhaps there was a code among these outlaws that they only steal cattle, not money. He shook his head. After years of chasing desperate men, he shouldn't be surprised about anything he came across. He handed a dollar to the young lady.

"Thank you for your kindness, *señorita."*

She shook her head. "Is all right, *señor.* I no need anything." She smiled and left.

Cyrus dressed and walked to the livery stable. Nothing would keep him from rescuing Mattie from her angry son.

By the time the posse made camp that first evening on the trail, every muscle in Cyrus' body ached. He wished he'd had time to wait another day or two before hitting the trail again. Taking Mattie away from there remained his motivation. He unsaddled his horse and carried his newly purchased bedroll to the outer edge of the encampment. The sun disappeared over the horizon and the men efficiently prepared camp, some gathering twigs for fire, others setting up small lean-tos, and several walking off the stiffness from the long ride.

Cyrus spread out his bedroll and lay flat on his back. He was tired and didn't feel like eating. Covering his eyes with his hat to filter out the light from the fire, he didn't wake up until the next morning.

Opening his eyes, he was surprised to discover the early morning predawn grayness. When he stood, his muscles were still stiff, but he felt better and was ready to hit the trail again. His stomach growled, reminding him of his missed supper. Eating first would be a good idea.

Eager to get back on the trail, the men didn't bother to cook anything for breakfast. They munched on whatever cold food they brought in their packs and broke camp before dawn.

The posse rode hard, occasionally stopping to water their horses and let them blow. During these periods, they'd grab something to eat. These men weren't much for talking during the day, but at night when they rested, they came alive with their talk of local politics and happenings in their town.

Cyrus listened to their friendly banter with interest. Sheriff Wilson and he had that kind of relationship once. He missed it. Cyrus longed to settle down long enough to get to know his neighbors. He wanted someone to talk to at the end of the day, someone to share his life with. A town to call his and a place of his own.

The yearnings made his thoughts turn once again toward Mattie. He hoped she hadn't suffered because of his escape. The moment Will found out she knew what kind of man he really was, he turned on her. His volatile personality became clear to everyone. Would Mattie be able to handle him?

So much time had passed since he left there. What happened? He guessed Will and the boys left home for a while so as not to get caught. Mattie wouldn't know where they were, of course. But he would talk her into getting out of there. He knew she would go with him when she heard his arguments. What would he use to get her to leave the canyon? Would she be willing simply because he wanted her to come with him? Would she marry him and help him build a new life on a little place somewhere? Did she love him?

Cyrus grew impatient to see Mattie. He wished he'd kissed her when he had the chance. He shouldn't have worried about what Will would say. The young man didn't come into the house that often anyway.

The trail spread out before him, seemingly endless. Cyrus would occasionally close his eyes a moment and daydream of what it would be like to kiss her and run his fingers through her pretty, dark blond hair.

His thoughts kept him company and drove him onward.

As the posse approached the hidden canyon, Cyrus held up a hand, motioning for them to stop. He apprised them of the whereabouts of the concealed guard in the rocks. They decided on a plan. The rocks and spires, identical in color to the canyon wall, would make it difficult to find the route used by the gang to reach the lookout spot.

Dismounting, Cyrus took another man with him to scout the rocks from above. They split up at the canyon mouth, each stalking opposite sides. Cautiously, the men crept along the sheer edge of the cliffs, peering below for signs of the sentinel. Cyrus couldn't see anyone and continued along the embankment. The scouts walked half a mile, signaling to one another they hadn't seen anyone in the rocks below, then finally returned to the rest of the posse.

"There's no one guarding the entrance," Cyrus reported to the sheriff. "It's peculiar. I don't know what to make of it, except they must have left when I disappeared. They're probably hiding out somewhere until it's safe to return."

The sheriff sighed. "If we came all this way…" He frowned at Cyrus and motioned to his men. "Mount up. We're going down there. Load your guns, and be ready for anything."

They spurred into action, and headed into the belly of the deep canyon. Every nerve in Cyrus' body tingled from heightened emotions. He knew the feeling well. His eyes darted from one side of the canyon to the other and back. They made it to the waterfall and left their horses behind, stealing the rest of the way on foot. Creeping around the last bend, guns drawn and ready, the posse entered the compound.

All was still. The sheriff motioned a group of men toward the bunkhouse and another to the cabin.

His finger on the trigger, Cyrus and two others rounded the corner of the house and retraced the steps he'd taken eight days before on his escape route. The air hung hot and silent as a church on Thursday. He crept onto the front porch and ducked under the window. Then, he kicked the door open and the three rushed inside, guns aimed at every corner of the room.

Nothing.

Nobody.

They searched the back bedrooms and found no one there, either. The others came to the cabin and reported that they hadn't found anyone. It appeared the gang had taken everything they could carry.

Cyrus checked Mattie's room. Most of her personal things were still there. All her clothes were gone.

"They've abandoned this hideout," Sheriff Tolaine said. Probably won't be coming back here again."

The words echoed in Cyrus' head. Never return? Where had they gone? Why did they take Mattie with them? His heart sank into his toes. This was his fault. It took him two years of tracking to locate the gang the first time. How long will it take him to find them again? And most importantly, was Mattie safe?

"We'll camp out here for the night. Then we've got to get back to town. There's no way we'll be able to track them out here." The sheriff gave Cyrus a look he couldn't quite read, but it definitely told him the lawman wasn't happy with the situation.

Cyrus wondered what to do next. There remained half a day of light. Should he head out and begin his search for the Gordon gang immediately? He was sick of the trail, and he was tired of bounty hunting. Except for finding Mattie, this was no longer worth his time or effort. Had she gone of her own will, or did they force her to go?

In the past, Will always left her home alone, not telling her where he was going, or making up a story about which state he would be in. He could have done that again. There wouldn't have been any need to take Mattie with him. He'd used her for nothing more than someone to cook his gang's meals and wash their clothes between jobs.

Then the realization hit him. He'd taken Mattie with him because they were never returning to this canyon. If Cyrus wanted to see her again, he'd have to hunt for the Gordon gang.

Why hadn't Mattie refused to leave with Will? He'd seen her stand up to him before. Cyrus searched the whole area to see if she might have left a note for him about their whereabouts, but he found nothing. He walked to the river and squatted down at the place where he jumped in to escape. Sticking his hands into the cool water, he swished it around.

Was God telling him this was how it should end? End of his

career, end of being in love. But he couldn't fall out of love that easily. He leaned against the side of the cabin and rubbed his forehead. This life was just too hard now. He wanted to end his bounty hunting days with a big reward, buy a little place, and settle down with a wife. Instead, he'd be leaving as a failure, having lost the only woman he'd ever loved. *Why, Lord? What am I supposed to do?*

Feeling the sheriff's empathy toward him, he sauntered back to his horse. Being new to his faith, trusting God was mighty difficult. But he'd give it a try.

Mattie told him God would have a personal relationship with him. Until now, he hadn't known exactly what she meant. God cared enough for him to guide his life. Cyrus knew in his heart what he must do.

He sought out the sheriff and extended his hand to him. "Thanks for acting on my tip. I'm sorry the hunt didn't turn out the way we'd like."

The sheriff shook his hand. "Don't worry about it. Sometimes tips pay off and sometimes they don't. It's part of the job."

Cyrus mounted his horse and rode out of the deep canyon, certain he'd never see this place again as long as he lived. The possibility was great that he'd never see Mattie again either. He raised his head with firm resolve to trust God. His bounty hunting days were over. A new life awaited him. It was time to get on with living it.

Chapter Nine

"Aren't you feeling well, Mother Gordon?" Bob turned in the doorway before following the men outside after supper. They'd taken over the abandoned farm before the first snow fell, after Will deemed the buildings solid enough to keep out the winter storms in Kansas.

"I'm fine, Bob. Thanks for asking."

"You haven't been yourself since we left the canyon."

Mattie stared into his brown eyes. How she longed for this kind of caring and attention from her son. But Will had turned cold toward her ever since she rode home with Cyrus.

"I appreciate your concern. You're a good man." She stacked dirty plates and carried them to the kitchen cupboard. "I'm feeling a little tired. I'm going to turn in as soon as I finish up here." How could she explain to Bob that she loved Cyrus and her heart ached for him? She might never see him again and prayed for him every night. Once in a while, doubt would settle in, leaving her hopeless. She sighed.

"I'll help you."

Mattie didn't turn down his offer. They worked side by side in comfortable silence. She was grateful Bob didn't attempt to cheer her up.

After finishing the dishes, he left the tiny house and Mattie worked on her needlework by the fireplace. When Will returned from overseeing something in the barnyard, he sat quietly by the fireplace, smoking his pipe and reading an old newspaper. The simple joys she previously treasured no longer held meaning for her: cooking and cleaning up after the men, watching their antics in trying to outshoot one another, sitting by a fire at night with her only son as a companion. Nothing brought her the peace she longed for.

Now she only did these things because she was obligated, compelled by the threat of harm if she didn't. In the past four months since finding this abandoned farm, Mattie tried countless times to speak to Will about giving his life to God, and each time she was met with an icy stare. All the men seemed to have turned against her, except Bob.

She jumped when a knock sounded on the door.

"Come in," Will called, looking up from his paper.

Jake peeked his head into the room. "We're all set, boss. Just need the provisions."

"Good. We'll be ready to ride after breakfast. Thanks." He returned to his reading.

"Where are you going?" Mattie already knew the answer, but she wanted Will to stop and think about how he was throwing away his life.

"Got a job to do. Money's low, and the boys are getting tired of sitting around this rotting, old place."

"Will, I wish you wouldn't—"

"Forget it, Mother." His voice hit her ears hard, like the sound of a frying pan dropping to the floor. "Don't waste your breath."

He stood, abandoning the paper in the chair and stretching

his arms. "Have a complete trail kit ready for us at dawn." He turned to walk out the door.

"Son!" she called out to him.

Will looked over his shoulder.

"Please be careful. I…love you."

"Yeah," he said dryly and left.

Mattie worked an hour past her bedtime preparing the necessary items for a long ride on the trail. She knew what she needed to do. Turn in her son and the gang before someone got hurt or killed. Mattie crawled into bed that night and cried into her pillow. She tried to pray, but the task grew difficult because of the heartbreaking duty ahead of her.

Lying awake long into the night, her thoughts shifted to Cyrus. Had he survived his escape from the canyon? Did he think about her as often as she thought about him? Would they ever find one another again?

Her heart heavy, she arose early the next morning and prepared breakfast. Her son hadn't learned anything from the dangers he'd faced. They only made him harder. The only way to save his life now would be to take it from him. Not by killing him, but by putting him in jail for a long time.

The men arrived for their morning meal with their usual noise and excitement, all except Conrad Baker. Instead of his usual upbeat demeanor, he wore a scowl and shot glares toward everyone in the room.

Eating their food like pigs, they then scattered to finish their preparations to leave. Two of them returned shortly and hauled the provisions out of the house. Others saddled their horses while Will and Jake squatted down in the yard, drawing a map on the ground with sticks. They spoke in hushed tones Mattie couldn't hear from the house.

Within fifteen minutes, the men were mounted and ready to go. Mattie watched the proceedings through the farmhouse window while washing and putting away the dishes.

They rode out of the yard like men with a purpose. Only Bob turned to look toward the house and wave at Mattie. Until Cyrus showed up in the canyon they all had done that, including Will.

Relieved to be alone once again, she finished cleaning the house and prepared to go into town. Stepping out onto the porch, she was startled by a deep voice coming from the shady part of the front porch.

"Well, now. You look like you're about to go somewhere." Conrad forced a smile. "I reckon I'll ride along with you." He glared at Mattie from where he sat, leaning against the house. She shrank back toward the doorway.

Will had known all along she would turn him in. No wonder Conrad had been upset that morning. No man would relish this kind of duty. She wondered how he came to be the one picked for the task.

"The boss suspected you might try something like finding that bounty hunter, or maybe turning us in to the law." He returned to his whittling. "I didn't figure you'd try it before lunch."

All Mattie's plans disintegrated. Destined to remain housebound, she smiled. Conrad had been with the gang for almost eight years, and she knew him pretty well. "Can't blame me for trying, can you?"

The corners of his mouth curled up. "Guess not. Just what were you planning to do?"

"You have a pretty good idea what I was going to do."

"Yeah. That's why Will left me here."

"We might as well make the best of it, since we're going to be together quiet a bit this month." Mattie pulled her bonnet off her head and turned to go back into the house. "How about some pie and coffee?"

"Sure." Conrad stood and followed her. He took a seat at the table to wait for his refreshment. "Why did you turn against us?"

"Against you? I'm not against you boys." It saddened her to think they felt that way about her. Was that what Will thought, too? "I care about you as I always have. Now that I know you've been on the wrong side of the law, it makes me responsible to the good citizens of this big country to keep you from hurting them."

"We never hurt anyone, not mortally anyway. And we only took from those who had so much they wouldn't have noticed anything missing."

"But that's wrong. Don't you see?" Mattie took a deep breath. She sliced a piece of pie and set it in front of Conrad. Then she poured two cups of coffee and took a seat across the table from him.

"I dunno. Maybe it's wrong. But we aren't hurting anyone by it."

"What about Will? They say he murdered a lady down in Texas."

"Will didn't kill that woman."

"How do you know that? I heard there were no witnesses other than the woman's husband."

"There was a witness."

"What?" Mattie felt her mouth drop open. "Who? Why didn't anyone come forward?"

"Fear."

Mattie thought she saw a glimmer of fright in the man's eyes. It only lasted a moment, then disappeared.

"If you know something that might get these charges against Will dropped, you must go to the authorities."

He sipped his coffee and shook his head. "Too dangerous. And it wouldn't make any difference. The witness is also a wanted man. Nobody would listen to him."

"Who is it?"

Silence.

"Conrad, who is the witness?"

He gulped the rest of his drink, set the cup on the table, and wiped his mouth on his sleeve. "I can't tell you that, Mother Gordon. It's too risky." He walked out the door, leaving Mattie to wonder about what he'd said.

If Conrad truly knew something about the incident in Texas that could get her son's charges dropped to cattle rustling and horse thieving, he must tell someone. How could only one gang member know when nobody else seemed to know anything about the shooting? She looked up with a start. Conrad must have witnessed the murder.

Her heart pounded like cracks of thunder on a rainy day. She had to get help. She had to let someone know her son was innocent. But how? If fear drove Conrad to silence all this time, then it would also compel him to guard her with everything in him.

The man whose wife Will was accused killing was a powerful man. She knew he'd have every lawman in Texas convinced Will was the murderer. Would anyone believe her, or would they listen to the lies circulating about Will? She needed someone who would believe her. Someone who trusted her. She needed Cyrus to help her, but she had no idea where he was, nor how to get a hold of him.

Mattie put her head down on the table, resting it on her arm. She had no way of getting help. How her heart ached to see Cyrus again. Why hadn't she allowed him to kiss her that night? She closed her eyes and imagined being in his arms, pretending she felt his heart beating beneath his waistcoat. A tear escaped her. She felt trapped. Alone. Useless. Helpless.

Her son could be exonerated from the murder charges, and she prayed for a way to get the news to the world. There were people out there hunting for Will; he was wanted dead or alive. She had to think of something.

If ever there was a time she needed to trust God, it was now. She prayed for Will. For Cyrus. For Conrad and the rest of the gang. She prayed for herself. Then she sat silently and listened to the still, small voice within her. An unusual assurance seeped into her soul and filled her with a new hope.

Mattie made several attempts to leave the old farmhouse during the next three weeks. Each time Conrad thwarted her efforts. For the first time in her life, she began to question God's plans for her life. Why would He allow her son to go free to steal what others worked hard to attain, when she, a Christian who did her best to live her life right, was held prisoner? Why wouldn't God allow her to use the new information about a possible witness in the murder case?

Weeks drug by until one day, while Mattie fried potatoes for supper, she looked up through the window and saw a wagon on the horizon, heading toward the farmhouse. Conrad sat on the porch steps, making certain his rifle was loaded, but acted as if he didn't have a care in the world. Mattie saw his keen eyes watching the approaching wagon.

The unmistakable clanking told her before the wagon arrived it was a peddler of goods. Conrad relaxed a bit, but never took his eyes off the man.

"Ho, there!" the driver called as he neared the house. He reined the horses to a stop and hopped down from the wagon. "I didn't know whether anyone bought this place or not. Glad to find someone here."

Mattie walked out onto the porch and the man approached her with confidence and a smile. He took her hand and kissed it. "I'm a simple peddler of goods, but for you, ma'am, I'll practically give away my store."

Mattie smiled. She hadn't seen a trader in a long time. She'd forgotten how smooth talking they were.

"May I trouble you good people for a dipper of water?"

"Yes, of course," Mattie said, looking toward Conrad. If he had any manners, he'd fetch the water, but she knew he wouldn't venture out of earshot of the dealer. "I'll be right back."

She rushed into the house and dunked the dipper into the pail. On her way out, she spied her pattern book, and a lump formed in her throat. A note. She could get a note to the local sheriff through the peddler.

Careful not to spill any water, she returned to the porch and handed it to the man. "Now, you sit on the porch with my son while I look over your wares."

Conrad's eyes shot her a strange look, but he said nothing. The peddler carried on a one-way conversation, and it seemed to Mattie he hadn't even noticed Conrad's unresponsiveness. She looked over the wares and chose several items they'd left behind when they moved from the canyon.

"Great choice." the man grinned. "I'll let you have the lot for two, fifty-five."

"I'll get the money, and be right back."

Mattie hurried into the house and quickly counted out the money. She scribbled a note on the corner of one of her pattern book pages and folded it in with the dollar bills. Returning to the porch, she placed the money into the man's hand. From what she remembered of peddlers, she knew he would never count the money in front of her. Showing trust to customers was the only way to gain repeat business.

She was right. He promptly stuffed the money into his trousers pocket and bowed to Mattie in a grand gentleman fashion. "Thank you, my lady. I will not take up any more of your time."

"You're welcome, sir. And thank you, too. Will we be seeing more of you around here?"

The man hoisted himself up onto the wagon seat. "You can be sure of that, ma'am. Good day."

Mattie and Conrad watched him go. Conrad finally relaxed when the man was out of sight. "Good thinking about calling me your son. That way he won't be suspicious."

"You were wound tighter than an old lady's hair bun in church on Sunday," she teased. "Now come inside. Supper's nearly ready."

The next morning, while Mattie fed Conrad his breakfast, the front door crashed open. Conrad pushed himself from the table, his chair collapsing behind him, and Mattie dropped the frying pan on the floor.

Three men rushed inside, their guns drawn. They aimed at Conrad's head. "Don't try anything, Mr.!" one man shouted. "Hands up in the air. We're the law, and you're under arrest for cattle rustling, horse thieving and kidnapping."

Conrad's face turned as white as Mattie's apron. His arms shot into the air. "What's this all about?"

"You're a member of the Will Gordon gang, and you're holding this here little lady prisoner." The man pointed toward Mattie. "We've come to take you in."

Conrad's mouth dropped open. Mattie swallowed hard. One man lowered his weapon and turned toward her. "Are you all right, ma'am?"

"Y…yes. I'm fine. He never hurt me."

The other two men handcuffed him and ushered Conrad outside. One kept him covered with his gun, while the other went to the barn to saddle a horse.

"That was mighty clever of you, sneaking that note to the peddler yesterday. Kinda frightened him, though." The man laughed. "I don't think he'll be around these parts much for quite some time." Then his smile disappeared and he frowned. "How do you know this man is part of the Gordon gang? And where are the rest of them?"

"Brace yourself, sheriff. I'm Will Gordon's mother."

The man's eyes grew wide as half dollar gold pieces and his mouth dropped open.

"I guess I'd better start at the beginning." Mattie offered him a chair at the table, and he accepted. She poured him some coffee and told him everything from the moment Cyrus drew a gun on her until the present.

The sheriff thanked her and headed outside. He mounted his horse. "Ma'am. I'm much obliged to you. I hope all goes well with you." They rode off toward town, Conrad's form slumping on his horse.

"I'll be praying for you, Conrad." she called after him. He turned toward her, an indiscernible look on his face. Mattie prayed someone would be able to get the information about witnessing the murder from him soon.

She cleaned up the dishes and packed some clothes, a bedroll and food. She saddled her horse and reined him toward town. Planning to talk to Conrad to see if he'd tell her more about witnessing the murder, she would then send a telegram to Sheriff Craig Wilson in Texas. Cyrus talked about him often, and maybe the sheriff would know where to find him.

Chapter Ten

Cyrus stared across the plains from the front porch of his little house. He didn't own it, but it was his as long as he kept up with the payments. How long had it been since he walked away from being a bounty hunter? Four months? It seemed longer.

He thought about the day he rode out of the canyon in Colorado, disappointed to find Mattie gone. Many times he'd been tempted to find her, but it would have put her in danger. He walked away from the bounty and from the only woman who'd ever gotten to him. Kin to an outlaw. He shook his head. Would she ever get out of his head or his heart?

Since first sneaking into the canyon and finding Mattie, his life had changed. He looked toward the northwest and remembered the last time he'd seen her standing on the porch in the moonlight, watching the scene in the yard with the bobcat. How he'd wanted to grab her and take her with him, get her out of that life and away from dangerous outlaws. But he knew they wouldn't both have made it. He had to think of her and let her stay in order to save her life, as well as his own.

Mattie, where are you? Are you safe?

Cyrus nearly drove himself insane with thoughts of her. He couldn't handle it anymore. This farm was nothing but emptiness without her. It could never be the dream he wanted if his heart remained broken and empty. He had to look for her. But where would he start? Who might know where the Gordon gang made their new hideout? It was certain they'd never go back to the canyon in Colorado.

Then he remembered Doc Lundine, the man in Kansas who knew where Will and the gang were at all times. Cyrus swallowed hard and rushed into the house. He packed as many items as his trail bags would hold. Hastily gathering his bedroll and a change of clothes, he rushed out to the barn to saddle his horse.

Stopping at the neighbor's to ask him to keep an eye on his place for him, he then he headed to Kansas for a clue as to where he could find the future Mrs. Cyrus Braydon.

Cyrus rode into Hays, Kansas tired, dirty and hungry. He boarded his horse and asked the stable boy where he could get a hot bath, food and a dry bed. The boy pointed down the street, and his eyes shone when he accepted the shiny penny he handed him.

Walking toward the Lamar Hotel, his excitement mounted at the thought of sleeping in a bed once again. He'd gone soft since signing the lease on the farm. There was a time when he hunted outlaws for months at a time without laying his head on a real pillow. His bones weren't young anymore. Settling down appealed to him more than he'd thought.

He checked into the hotel, took a lukewarm bath in water used only once, and dressed in his clean suit of clothes. After leaving his dirty ones with the laundress, he stepped out into the street. How would he find the doctor without arousing suspicion?

The best place for that would be a saloon. Looking up and down the street, he easily spotted several. Cyrus swallowed hard. What would God think of him going into one of those lairs? Somehow, he knew it would be fine. God accepted him the way he was, not the most perfect man on earth. He'd made his share of mistakes and drank his share of hooch. That was all behind him now.

I got a feeling Mattie's in some sort of trouble, Lord. And the best place I know where men have loose tongues is in the saloon. Now I'm not going to do anything You won't approve of while I'm there, so I'd appreciate if You'd help me find this doctor real quick. Amen.

Once inside the swinging doors, Cyrus stepped up to the bar. He asked for a cup of coffee. The bartender poured the thick, dark liquid into a cup and slid it toward him. "You got some sort of ailment keeping you from drinking like a man?"

Cyrus chuckled. "I don't know if I'd call it an ailment, but yeah, I got something that prevents me from drinking. You wouldn't happen to know of any doctors in this town, would you?"

"Sure. We got us several fine doctors." The man grinned, displaying a missing front tooth. "There's old Doc Suthers, and then there's Doc Perton." The man scratched his head, a puzzled look on his face. He looked up and called to the other side of the room. "Hey, Manny, what's the name of that new doctor in town, the young one?"

"Trenton," A man answered.

"Yeah, that's it. Doc Trenton."

Cyrus' heart sank. No Doc Lundine. Maybe the man moved on when he found out the Gordon gang had been discovered. He might have figured he'd get caught too. Should he ask outright whether they know Doc Lundine? Deciding it might throw suspicion on him, Cyrus paid the man for his coffee and went outside, glad to leave the darkness of the den-like room.

Where should he continue his search? Walking down the street, he noticed the ornamental sign on the tonsilory parlor boasting of haircuts, shaves, and tooth extraction. That's it. Maybe he's not looking for a physician, but rather a dentist. He headed straight for the parlor and walked inside. Several men looked up and nodded.

"I'll be with you soon as I can," the barber told him. "Been pretty busy in here today."

"I can wait," Cyrus answered. Taking a seat near the door, he picked up a very worn newspaper and began to read. The barber prattled on with his customers and finally called Cyrus to the metal chair with dark red velvet cushions.

"What can I do for you today?"

"Shave, please."

The man quickly lathered Cyrus' face. He sharpened his razor on a leather strap and began shaving him. It felt good to be spoiled a bit. A barber hadn't shaved him for quite some time.

When finished, Cyrus stood and rubbed his smooth chin. He reached into his pocket, pulled out a dime and tossed it to the man. "Great job, Mr.—"

"Blaylock. Thanks." The man grinned. "Be sure to tell everyone I give the best shave in town."

"I'll do that." Cyrus sighed. Another dead end. He put his hat on and started out the door. A man of medium height and portly build bumped into him on his way out. He scowled at Cyrus. "Excuse me." Cyrus tipped his hat and brushed passed the important looking businessman.

"Mr. Lundine," Cyrus heard the barber say. "Perfect timing. My chair just opened up."

Cyrus stopped in his tracks. Lundine. His heart raced. Spinning on his heels, he returned to the shop and picked up the newspaper he'd been reading. "Hey, Mr. Blaylock," he called. "Mind if I take this paper with me?"

"Help yourself," the man replied. "It's too old to even charge you for it."

"Thanks." Cyrus exited the shop, the face of the man called Lundine imprinted firmly in his mind.

He crossed the street and sat on a bench in front of the hardware store. Opening the paper, he held it out as if reading, all the while keeping an eye on the tonsilory parlor. A half hour later, he watched the man come out of the shop. Mr. Lundine took out his pocket watch, opened it, and replaced it in his sophisticated waistcoat pocket.

He walked down the boardwalk and Cyrus trailed him to the Cattlemen's Association building. At the door, Cyrus was stopped by a huge gentleman, wearing a fancy, pinstriped suit.

"This club is for members and their guests only."

"I'm a guest of Doc Lundine."

The man's eyebrows raised. He opened the door wide for Cyrus to pass. "Third door on the right, upstairs."

"Thanks, good man." He walked through a hallway and up the stairs. The doors bore the names of various men, and he stopped in front of the third one on the right. Printed in large, gold lettering was the name, Chester Lundine, President.

He knocked.

"Come in."

Cyrus squared his shoulders and entered the room. He'd seen few places in his lifetime that could compare with this one in its pure opulence.

The man he'd seen in the barbershop stood to his feet from behind a huge, walnut desk. "Who are you? How did you get in here?"

"Are you Doc Lundine?"

The man's face didn't change expressions, but his eyes widened considerably. "Where'd you get the idea I'm a doctor?"

"From a mutual acquaintance."

"Who?" the man demanded.

"Someone in the Gordon family."

The man cleared his throat and motioned for Cyrus to sit in an overstuffed leather chair across the desk from him. Then he offered him a cigar, which Cyrus refused.

"Now," Mr. Lundine leaned back in his chair and puffed on his cigar. "Suppose you tell me what this is all about."

Years of thinking fast helped Cyrus know what to say. "You know the Gordons had to move because of some bounty hunter locating their canyon hideout."

Mr. Lundine didn't respond. Cyrus cleared his throat and continued. "I've known Mattie Gordon for some time, and I need to find her. She has something that belongs to me." It wasn't a lie. Mattie held his heart.

"What does all this have to do with me?"

"I know you have knowledge of how to find the Gordons, and I came to ask you for your help."

"Mr., I don't know who you are, nor do I care. I don't know what you're talking about, and I want you out of my office, now."

Cyrus could tell by the man's voice and the veins standing out in his neck that he'd gone too far. He'd never tell him where the Gordons were. Mr. Lundine stood and walked over to the door. Opening it, he motioned for Cyrus to leave.

"Thank you for your time, doc. If you should remember anything, let me know. I'm staying at the Lamar Hotel. Room 14."

Cyrus stepped out of the office. The door slammed behind him. He walked downstairs and out into the sunshine. He was angry with himself for not handling the situation better. *You've lost your touch. That didn't go well at all.*

Later that evening after supper, Cyrus sat in his room, reading a newspaper he'd bought that afternoon. He put the paper in his lap and reached over to the nearby table for a glass of water, when he noticed something unusual under the door. The small stream of light from the hallway was interrupted by two dark shadows. Slipping quietly across the room, he grabbed his rifle and pressed his back to the wall behind the door and waited, watching the shadows on the floor. The shadows moved away. Cyrus couldn't hear any footsteps. Was he sneaking away, or still waiting for him to leave the room?

He stood there for what seemed like an hour before deciding to move. With one swift move, he lunged for the doorknob and pushed open the door. Jumping into the hallway, he drew his rifle, ready for firing. Nobody was there. Feeling a little foolish, he returned to his room. Leaving his rifle and locking the door, he went downstairs to the desk.

"I'd like to get a room close to mine for a lady who should be arriving sometime tonight."

"Certainly, sir. Please sign her name here."

Cyrus wrote a name in the registry and took the key from the Manager. "Room seventeen across the hall and down one door from yours."

"Thanks."

He returned to his room, packed up his few belongings and cautiously moved to the room he requested for Margie Anderson. That was a name he hadn't thought of in ages. The little redheaded girl from school. Certain Mr. Lundine wouldn't catch on to his trick, he lay on the bed in room seventeen with his rifle loaded right beside him. He didn't sleep much.

Sometime after midnight Cyrus heard light footsteps in the hallway. Sneaking to the door, he placed his ear against it to listen. He heard the sound of a key being jiggled in a lock and then the creek of a door opening.

"He's not here," A male voice said quietly.

"He's gotta be. No one saw him leave."

"Look for yourself."

Cyrus heard some shuffling and then nothing.

"What are we gonna tell Mr. Lundine? He'll be furious at us for letting him get away."

"How should I know? I never wanted to get mixed up with the Gordon gang in the first place."

"Shhh."

"Aw, shh yourself. I'm getting out of here. There's something strange afoot. Ever since that gang moved to Liberal, Mr. Lundine's been on edge."

"Yeah. He looked worried. That's why he wanted us to take care of this fella."

The two voices disappeared down the hallway. Nobody would be that foolish as to mention names out in the open for anyone to hear. Cyrus went back to bed. Someone wanted him to think the Gordons are in Liberal. He knew why. To throw him off the trail. There's no mistake about who that someone was, Doc Lundine. He was the only person Cyrus talked to about the Gordon gang since arriving in town. The man definitely lied to him about knowing Will Gordon. He wasn't a doctor, but a cattleman. That must be the connection to Will. Perhaps Lundine purchased Gordon's stolen cattle at low prices, then sold them at a profit. How did he get away with it? All this thinking was giving him a headache. He closed his eyes, formulating a plan before falling asleep.

Awaking to dawn's soft glow, Cyrus sat up and rubbed his eyes. Excited, he jumped out of bed and dressed quickly. He got some breakfast in the hotel dining room, then checked out of both rooms. Walking briskly to the stable, he kept his trained eyes looking around town. His keen senses told him he was being watched. The sound of boots clopping behind him on the boardwalk, stopping whenever he did. A figure ducking into doorways whenever Cyrus turned to look into a store window. This shadow was not a professional. If he was, he wouldn't be so easily detected.

After paying the stable hand, he saddled his horse, and rode out of town. Heading north toward Liberal, he pushed onward through the day and camped at night. His keen tracking instincts told him he'd been followed half the day, and then left alone. The plan worked.

The next morning he rode to the stage stop he'd passed on his way to Hays and bought a used hat and coat. Then he rented a fresh horse, which was hard to get used to, having ridden Shadow all those years of tracking outlaws. He hoped the new clothes and horse would throw suspicion off him when he rode back into Hays. He'd return to get Shadow in about a week if all went well. The thought of reuniting with his trusted friend brought a smile to his face. The animal has certainly earned some rest.

Cyrus stopped at the edge of town and got a room at a boarding house under the name of Ben Cord. Ben was his father's name and Cord he got from looking at a cord of firewood nestled against the side of the house.

Mrs. Crandell, the widow who ran the boarding house, treated him well and fed him until he thought his waistcoat buttons would pop open. He spent his days wandering around town with his head held low and hat brim covering his eyes. Cyrus eyed every person he passed without them knowing it. Nothing went on in Hays that he didn't know about. But all his efforts brought him nothing but another headache.

Late one afternoon, while sitting on the boarding house porch sipping strong coffee, he noticed a strange cloud forming on the horizon. Having spent years on the trail, he soon recognized it as a cattle drive. He estimated they would arrive in town in about two more hours, just as the sun would be ready to set. Keeping an eye on the cloud, Cyrus noticed it began to dissipate. They were stopping already? No cattle boss would stop a drive when this close to a major shipping yard.

His heart beat faster. Perhaps this is what he'd been waiting for. It might be the Will Gordon gang. He rushed into the house to tell Mrs. Crandell he wouldn't be there for supper, then ran to the corral behind the barn and saddled the rented horse. Within minutes, Cyrus galloped north toward the spot where he last saw the cloud of dust, hoping for a clue to help him find Mattie.

Chapter Eleven

Mattie took a deep breath and walked into the sheriff's office. "I wish to see Conrad Baker."

"You mean the man who held you against your will?" The deputy shook his head. "You're crazy, lady."

"I may be crazy," Mattie said as she removed her gloves, "but you should know not to cross a mother on a mission."

The deputy smiled crookedly and motioned for Mattie to follow him to the back of the building. He led her to the jail cells, and she was grateful they'd been cleaned recently. Lawrence, one of her son's men, once told her the stench from just one night of drunks could overpower an average person. He probably knew about it from spending time in a jail. Mattie shook her head. Why hadn't she noticed these clues before?

"Baker," the deputy said. "You got a visitor."

Mattie's heart beat hard in her chest as she walked up to the cell. Conrad stood and came to the bars, his brows furrowed, his eyes raging tornadoes. "Why'd you do it? You've ruined my life."

Mattie hadn't seen such anger from this young man before. It surprised her. "I did it for your own good."

"Ha! My own good. How many people wreck other's lives for their own good?"

"Conrad, you know it was a matter of time before the whole gang would get caught, maybe even killed. This way you at least get to live."

"Unless they hang me," he said wryly.

Mattie shuddered. The ugly thought had occurred to her before, but she'd put it out of her mind. Nor did she care to think about it now. She lowered her voice as much as possible to keep others in the jailhouse from overhearing. "You've got to tell me about the other witness to that murder. If you know anything that could save Will's life, I beg you to tell me. Please."

"It doesn't matter now. Nobody would believe an outlaw, especially one who's worked for Will for eight years."

"I would. And I think there are a few others, too. You might be surprised."

"I'm not gonna talk until I know my last day's near."

"I love my son, and I don't want him to die without knowing his Savior." She reached through the bars and touched the work-worn hand of the man who'd been her captor for the past three weeks. "Please."

He looked down at her hand, then into her eyes. For the first time, she saw his weariness. Conrad's gaze darted around the jailhouse. Then he leaned into the bars. She could barely hear his next words. "I'm the witness."

Mattie suspected this from their conversation back at the farmhouse, but hearing it directly from him lifted her spirits. Her son was not a murderer.

She smiled at him. "Thank you. Were you afraid to come forward because they'd know you're one of the gang?"

"Nope."

Mattie furrowed her brows. "Then why?"

"I was supposed to be guarding the door the afternoon Will

visited Sarah Tarner. I looked through the kitchen window and saw a plate of cookies on the table. I went inside to grab one and it tasted good, and stood there feeding myself for a few minutes." He lowered his voice even more, and Mattie turned her ear to hear him. "Then I heard the front door open and I ducked into the pantry. Mr. Tarner had come home. I had to tell Will, so I snuck up the back staircase, hoping to find him before Tarner did. When I got to the main hallway, I peeked around the corner in time to see Tarner open a door. A lady screamed, 'No! Bill, don't shoot him!'"

"I heard a shot and Tarner yelled, 'Sarah, no! I didn't mean it.'"

Conrad swallowed before continuing his story. "Will ran out of the room. His gun was still in his holster. I rushed down the back stairs, and around to the front of the house. Will was fighting mad at me. The look on his face made me think he could have shot me if we didn't need to get away quick. Anyway, I told him I had to use the outhouse for only a second and that's why I left my post. He believed me. I've been scared of what Will would do to me if he ever found out I not only let him down, but I lied to cover my own skin. Will hates cowards."

Mattie patted his hand. "I'll see you get a fair trial. Remember, God can give you peace for your weary, frightened soul."

"Time's up," the deputy's voice interrupted them from somewhere behind Mattie.

She reached up to Conrad's face and drew it downward and kissed his cheek. "Where's Will now?" she asked softly.

"I guess there's no getting out of here now. I might as well tell you. He'd be on his way to Hays. Are you gonna turn him in too?"

She nodded her head, and left the building. She needed to find Cyrus fast. Knowing Will's approximate location, Mattie was certain he could catch up with him and get him into jail. Getting the murder charges dropped became her main concern, before someone took the wanted poster seriously and killed Will. Regardless of the outcome of all of this, she wanted two things: another chance to tell Will about Jesus' forgiveness and for everyone to know her son is not a murderer.

Walking into the telegraph office, she composed a note to Sheriff Wilson, then got a room at the hotel. After pacing the floor of her room for quite some time, she finally went downstairs to the lobby to locate a newspaper to occupy her time.

The next morning she checked for messages from Texas. The operator handed her one. She thanked him and left. Tearing open the envelope, she read the missive.

Mrs. Gordon, Cyrus hung up his guns about four months ago **stop** *Got a little place outside Waco Texas* **stop** *Sheriff Craig Wilson* **stop-end.**

Mattie composed another note to send to Cyrus in Waco.

Cyrus, have a witness proving Will didn't kill that girl **stop** *Come to Scott City Kansas* **stop** *Need your help* **stop** *Mattie* **stop-end.**

Cyrus dismounted his horse when close enough to see the group of men preparing their camp. He stayed an adequate distance away from the herd so no one would see him. Hiding in a small clump of bushes on the edge of a dry creek bed, he waited until dark before sneaking in for a closer look at the drovers. Counting six men around the campfire and three watching the herd, it didn't take him long to recognize them as the Gordon gang.

One was missing. He'd have to watch out for that one. Carefully, he returned to the bushes and hunkered down to try to get some sleep. Only a half a mile between him and three thousand dollars. He'd promised Mattie he would take Will in alive. There was no telling whether the law in Hays was corrupt. Having traveled these plains for years, he knew Hays was in the process of being tamed. But men like Lundine usually bribed the local law in order to get more of whatever they wanted. These underhanded criminals, living dual lives, were worse than all the Will Gordons in the world. At least with Will, one knew what he was. It's the sneaks who caused the most problems, hiring people like Gordon in order to keep their 'good' names in tact.

They all disgusted him. Cyrus wished he knew a way to rid the earth of all vermin who preyed on the innocent. Then a twinge of guilt squeezed his heart. He knew that was God's job, not his.

Lord, all I want is to find Mattie, make her my bride and settle down. I can't see getting this close to a gang of outlaws without having them arrested. Yet if I let them go, they'll head home. And home is where I'll find Mattie. Please guide me, Lord and show me what to do. Amen.

Leaning against the side of the dry creek bed, he rested his chin against his chest and dozed off. The next morning, Cyrus awoke with a start. He'd dreamed Mattie was in trouble and needed his help, but he couldn't find her. Hoping this wasn't a foreshadowing of events to come, he dusted himself off and hopped onto his horse. He didn't head for Hays, but rather another town twenty miles away. The only person he could trust was his old friend, Sheriff Craig Wilson. He needed the man's expert advice on this situation.

Later that day, he rode into the small cow town and stopped in front of the telegraph office. Once inside, he took care in composing the message.

Need advice **stop** *sitting on top of WG* **stop** *Need to locate his mother* **stop** *Sticky local situation* **stop** *WG knows mother's whereabouts* **stop** *Never been in this position before* **stop** *Awaiting your reply* **stop** *Cyrus* **stop-end.**

Cyrus hoped he'd given Craig enough to go on, but not enough for the locals there in Oklahoma to become alerted. He went to the town's only hotel and got a bunk in a room with three other men. After supper, he turned in early.

The next morning, it surprised him that he'd gotten any sleep at all. The other three men had stumbled into the room in the middle of the night, throwing their belongings on the floor. When they finally settled in their bunks, one snored like a two-man cross saw.

Cyrus headed straight for the telegraph office. It wasn't open yet, so he walked across the street to a place with a sign that read Clara's Restaurant for some breakfast. As soon as he finished, he returned to the telegraph office. No message yet.

Cyrus hated waiting. Who knew how quickly the Gordon gang might complete their transaction. With Doc Lundine knowing someone was looking for Mattie through Will, he may have tipped them off and they might already be gone. He paced up and down the small town. Sitting on a bench in front of the local mercantile made him fidgety.

"Mr. Braydon!"

Cyrus looked across the street and saw the telegraph operator running across the street, a note in his hand. "It arrived!"

He stood and the man handed him the note.

"I knew you were mighty anxious to get this, so I came lookin' for ya."

"Thanks. I appreciate it." He pulled a dime out of his pocket and tossed it to the fellow.

"Thanks, Mr. Braydon. Good luck to ya." The man took off down the street, whistling.

Cyrus tore open the note.

Cy, got telegram from her last week asking for your whereabouts **stop** *Came from Scott City Kansas* **stop** *Told her you were in Waco* **stop** *Dispatched Texas' best rangers to help with WG situation* **stop** *Sit tight* **stop** *If he moves, leave word there* **stop** *Will most likely head home to Mama* **stop** *Will intercept* **stop** *Sheriff Wilson* **stop-end.**

Mattie was looking for him. Was it was possible she loved

him and missed him? He groaned at the thought she may practically be at his place in Texas by now.

Cyrus owed it to her to make sure the Texas Rangers, dispatched by Sheriff Wilson, didn't kill her only son. He checked out of the hotel and headed back to the site where he'd seen the gang camped the night before.

As he neared the place, he was surprised and relieved to discover they were still there. Spying on them from the creek bed, he watched for a couple hours. Then he heard thundering hooves, and looking to the south, saw a dozen riders fast approaching the site. The Gordon gang rose to their feet, but no one drew guns.

The newcomers rode into camp and dismounted. They shook hands and patted one another on the back. Cyrus didn't recognize any of the new riders. He'd hoped to catch Doc Lundine at some foul play, but Lundine wasn't with them. The sneaky coward.

The cowboys sat around the fire, talking. Cyrus wished he could get closer, but knew it would be impossible without getting caught. He was already too close.

After about an hour of talking, the men split up. The Gordon gang saddled up and rode toward the southwest. The others took control of the herd. Cyrus crawled backward on his hands and knees until he was out of sight. Mounting his horse, he took off after Will.

The gang bypassed the little town Cyrus stayed in the night before, but Cyrus stopped long enough to leave word at the sheriff's office that Will appeared to be heading toward Scott City. Then he easily found their trail and began tracking them, the bounty hunter inside taking over the farmer in him.

Mattie paced the floor of the rundown farmhouse outside Scott City for the sixth day in a row. Conrad was safe from hanging for now because the judge, figuring to capture a bit of notoriety, decided to wait until the entire gang was in custody. He wanted to try them together in one big show of the law. But time was running out. Will said he'd be gone for a month. It would be exactly a month in a couple more days. In the past he was rarely off by more than a day or two in his estimations.

If Conrad was so afraid of Will that he'd kept from him the fact he'd been a witness to what happened that day in Texas, then what was her son capable of doing? Would he murder, even though he claimed to have never mortally wounded anyone?

Why hadn't Cyrus answered her telegram? Now that he'd retired from bounty hunting, did he want to forget everything about his previous life? She thought he cared for her, maybe even loved her. Now she wasn't sure. Yet he was the only person she knew who would believe her about the witness. While everyone around Scott City prepared for Will's return, Mattie knew it was possible he might not make it home alive. She needed someone to help save her son.

Lord, help me. I don't know what to do. Cyrus won't answer me, and Will is due back within a week. Why did You bring Cyrus into my life only to turn it upside down? Where is Your justice, Lord? What about all those prayers I've prayed for Will? Did you not hear them? Please, Lord. I need answers. I need Your help now.

Mattie lay on her bed and let the tears flow down to her pillow. Then her mind began to work. Perhaps if she went out and intercepted Will, they could go somewhere else until she had time to figure out how to get the charges dropped. She would have to do this without Cyrus Braydon's help. She had God on her side. He would help her. He would understand this was only a temporary detour before Will would be imprisoned for a long time. At least he would remain alive. As long as he had breath, Mattie maintained hope that he might give his heart to the Lord.

Mattie pushed the gnawing thought about hanging out of her mind and scurried around the little house, gathering things like a squirrel preparing for winter. She tied as much as she could onto the back of her horse, then mounted up and left. Until they caught Will, they wouldn't do anything to Conrad. He'd be safe, as well as the precious testimony that might save her son's life.

With a prayer in her heart for guidance, Mattie headed east, the opposite direction from the town. No one would know she left.

She camped out under the stars that night. Having grown up in Missouri, the outdoors didn't frighten her. Both her father and her husband enjoyed taking her camping. While many women were fearful of the vast western frontier, she embraced it. That's why she had been content to live in the little box canyon in Colorado all those years. Until Cyrus barged into her life, Mattie had everything she wanted and needed. Now she realized she missed the company of someone her own age. Someone to share her life with. No. She had to stop that line of thinking. Cyrus hadn't answered her request for help. He didn't care for her like she cared for him.

The next morning before the sun was straight overhead, she saw riders coming toward her in the distance. When they got within a quarter of a mile, she knew it was Will and the boys.

"What are you doing here?" Will pulled up beside Mattie, a scowl on his face. "Where's Con?"

"He's in jail." She watched his face become like an angry storm cloud. "I figured you'd be coming home soon, and thought I'd better come warn you. They're waiting for you."

He stared at her for a moment. Nodding, he turned toward the others. "We're heading North, men. The law's on to us. Con's in jail."

They spurred their horses north. Bob pulled up to Mattie. "Are you all right, Mother Gordon?"

She smiled at him and nodded. "I'm fine. Maybe a little tired from all this worrying about everyone."

He reached over and patted her hand. "You're a good woman. You deserve better than this." Then he turned and followed the rest of the gang.

Mattie took a drink from her canteen, rubbed her horse's neck, and then followed after the outlaw gang. With so many people after Will now, she had to keep an eye on her son.

Chapter Twelve

The tracks puzzled Cyrus. Why had Will suddenly headed north when only a day and a half from Scott City? Back in Hays he counted only nine of them. He knew from months of tracking, there were ten in the gang. Now it appeared a tenth man joined up with them. Perhaps Will left a scout or guard behind. There must be trouble brewing in town.

Cyrus searched the horizon, weighing his options. He'd head to Scott City immediately if he thought Mattie was there, but she had apparently gone to Texas to look for him. Now the gang was moving farther north, farther away from Mattie. When she found out he wasn't at his home in Texas, would she stay there? Was she waiting for him now? All this thinking made his head throb.

Cyrus glanced behind him. Where were those Texas Rangers? When they catch up to him, he planned to turn the bunch of criminals over to them and head to Texas to find his true love. He smiled. This was beginning to sound like one of those dime novels.

Cyrus turned north and continued tracking. He'd ridden another two hours when the rangers caught up to him. Explaining to them that all ten men were heading north, he requested if at all possible, they take Gordon alive.

The ranger in charge of the posse gave Cyrus a puzzled look. "I can't guarantee that. The poster said dead or alive."

"I know," Cyrus said, squinting toward the north. "But I promised his mother I'd do my best to see Will Gordon doesn't get killed."

The man shifted in his saddle and cleared his throat. "Like I said, I can't give my word on it, but I'll spread the word to my men. That's about all I can do. Thanks for you help. You can pick up your portion of the reward money in Abilene, Texas."

Cyrus had forgotten about the reward money. Did he even want it now? He tipped his hat to the ranger and spurred his horse south to Abilene.

Mattie watched Bob catch up to Will ahead of her. They stopped their horses and talked. She rode up beside them.

"You set us up, didn't you?" The veins in Will's neck stuck out.

"No." Mattie shook her head, shocked to hear her son's venomous accusation.

"You told them to follow you, and you led them straight to us. You're probably in cahoots with that bounty hunter again, aren't you? How long after we left did you wait before turning Conrad in?"

"You've got it all wrong, Will—"

He slapped her face, nearly knocking her off her horse. Mattie cradled her cheek in her hand, the shock of what her son did splintered her heart in two.

"I'll never forgive you for this, Mother. Now ride." He smacked her horse's rump with his quirt, and the gang took off at a full gallop.

Mattie couldn't think of anything except staying on the horse, the sting on her cheek reflecting the pain in her heart. There was no time to brush back the tears in her eyes, and they streaked down her face freely. She rode hard. Soon, dirt and dust mingled with the water on her cheeks. Giving her horse the rein, she followed the others across the prairie.

Was this the Lord's answer to her prayers? No. Don't give in to the tricks of the enemy. She'd chosen to trust Him, and she wouldn't stop now.

The next hour was a blur of prairie dust for Mattie. She held on to the reins and kept up with the gang. Then, in an instant she felt herself falling forward over the horse's head. Her horse whinnied. She landed facedown in the dirt and skidded along the earth. The horse rolled across her back.

There was nothing but dirt in her eyes, nose and mouth. She could smell it and taste the soil mixed with blood.

Then there was nothing at all.

Mattie drifted in a world between sleep and wakefulness. Spinning in a dark void, she couldn't open her eyes. Her arms wouldn't move. She could feel nothing, yet pain became her constant companion. Distorted voices echoed in her head whenever she tried to focus on them. They caused her to rotate in circles of blackness. Then the whirling stopped, and she again drifted into nothingness.

Eventually, Mattie awoke to realism. She felt the softness of a featherbed beneath her back.

A soft, gentle song floated through the gauzy wrappings. Mattie tried to speak, but her mouth felt as if it were swollen shut. She moaned. The singing stopped, and someone placed a hand on her shoulder.

"Are you awake, dearie?"

Mattie moaned.

"I'll be right back." The woman sounded excited.

Mattie heard the tapping of heels across a wooden floor and the creaking of door hinges. Momentarily, someone with heavier footsteps entered the room. She looked at the people with her left eye, but it wouldn't open very far, so she closed it again.

"Sarah tells me you're awake," a deep, masculine voice said. "Good thing I was still here. I'm Dr. Jennings. You gave us quite a scare, ma'am."

"Where am—" Mattie started to speak, but her face hurt too much to continue.

"Don't try to talk yet. You had a bad fall. I was on my way here when I saw you go down." He patted her shoulder. "Do you remember the accident?"

Mattie tried to think. She remembered riding hard with Will and the men. Her horse fell. It all happened in a moment. She nodded.

"Good. At least you don't appear to have any memory problems," the doctor said and took her wrist. "Often, this kind of injury to the head causes lapses in memory. Your pulse is good." He gently placed her arm back onto the bed.

How badly am I hurt? What happened to Will? Is he still alive?

"You're at my sister's home. She's a good nurse. That's the lady you met a moment ago."

"Hello again. I'm Sarah," she heard the gentle voice say. "It'll be no trouble at all taking care of you, dearie. I've nursed many people back to health. And my brother is the best doctor this side of the Mississippi."

"I'll tell you what happened to you," the doctor's voice came from a different spot in the room. "You evidently skidded on the right side of your face. You have a lot of lesions and bruises. Your right arm and wrist is broken, and three right ribs are bruised. Your jaw locked up, and your right hand also has several breaks. It will take time for you to heal."

No. It can't be that bad. A sob escaped from her throat, and a sharp pain shot through her jaw. The doctor touched her shoulder. "There, there. We're going to help you through this. You're going to be all right. It's just going to take time."

How long would it be before she could communicate with anyone? When would she be able to ask about Will? Her heart ached to know if he was all right. Did the boys know where she was? Did anyone care?

Would Will care? She remembered the last time he talked to her, the sting from his slap still fresh in her mind. No. He wouldn't be concerned.

Cyrus didn't care either. He hadn't answered her plea for help.

She was all alone now.

Nobody would come for her.

The doctor said she needed time. Time was all she had left in the world.

No. That wasn't true. She still had God. Despite all that happened, He would always be there for her. He would be her friend. She prayed for His will to be done concerning her son, and she knew God was still at work. Mattie sighed deeply. It felt as if God gave her a hug.

Maybe the doctor was right. She would be all right.

Cyrus couldn't believe the telegram he held in his hand from Mattie.

The operator told him it arrived around the middle of the month. That would be about the time he was in Hays. Mattie had turned to him when she needed help, and he wasn't there. Instead, he was out chasing her son again. He had only one option, hit the trail once more.

Cyrus left Waco and made good time, arriving in Scott City one day less than he expected. Driven by the thought of seeing the woman he loved, he rode into town and stopped at the local sheriff's office.

He strode into the jail.

"Hello," the sheriff greeted him. "What can I do for you?"

"I'm looking for the whereabouts of Mattie Gordon."

"Mattie Gordon?" the sheriff stood and walked from behind his desk. "Would that be Will Gordon's mother?"

"Yes. That's her."

"Nobody's seen her since before the shootout."

"Shootout?" *Oh, no.* He should have been there. He promised Mattie he'd make sure nothing happened to Will. Now it looked like he'd let her down.

"Yeah, some Texas Rangers caught up with the Gordon gang and surrounded them. But they didn't give up easy. Three wounded, three dead."

"Will Gordon?"

"Wounded in the leg. After the doctor declared him well enough to travel, they extradited him down to Abilene, Texas, to stand trial for murder."

"I need to find Mattie Gordon. She has evidence that Will didn't commit that murder."

"Well, now. That's interesting. But like I said, nobody's seen her since they caught Conrad Baker."

"Thanks for your help, sheriff. If you hear anything, please send a telegram to Sheriff Craig Wilson in Waco, Texas."

The man wrote the name down. "I'll do that."

Cyrus walked out into the sunshine. Lord, You've got to help me find her. Maybe he should send a telegram to Abilene to see if she followed Will down there. He'd never sent so many telegrams in his life. And waiting drove him crazy. But it would be best not to go back to Texas until he knew for certain she was there.

Cyrus paced the floor as he'd been doing for the past three days. No word from Texas. Then a knock came at the door. He opened it. The telegraph operator held out an envelope to him. He tossed him a nickel and tore open the message.

*Braydon, haven't seen Mrs. Gordon or son **stop** Will keep eye open for her **stop-end.***

If not there, then where had she gone? Cyrus swatted the back of a chair, sending it crashing to the floor. How had things become so confusing? Helping her son meant a lot to her. She'd asked for his help. But now she'd disappeared.

For the first time in his life, Cyrus had no idea what he should do or where he should go. He dropped to his knees by the bed, something he'd never done before.

"Lord, I've never been one to ask for help, but I sure could use some now. I don't know how things got so mixed up. Please help me find Mattie. You know she's become very important to me. And thanks for touching my life. I know You've probably got a lot more work to do on me, but I plan to be around for a long time. Please protect Mattie, wherever she is. Thanks."

When he stood, Cyrus felt peaceful and calm; completely opposite of what he expected. He stood in awe for a moment, basking in the Lord's presence. With it came the assurance that God remained in control of his life.

The peace stayed with him when he went to the sheriff's office to look for further clues that might tell him where Mattie was.

* * *

Mattie dreaded waking up from her naps. Often the pain in her body became unbearable. She'd blacked out from it a couple times. The nurse gave her regulated doses of laudanum, which helped, but there was no real way to convey to her that it wasn't enough.

When she could withstand the pain, Mattie prayed for Will and the boys, for herself, and she even prayed for Cyrus, although she knew he didn't return her love. Perhaps he might remain a good friend. They could write letters. Mattie didn't want to grow old alone.

How she wished she knew what happened to Will. If he were imprisoned, she could move close by and visit him whenever allowed. As long as he had breath, she knew there was hope for him to accept Jesus' forgiveness for his sins.

She opened her eye every now and then and caught a glimpse of Sarah. The woman was plain but had a nice face. Sleeping so often, she couldn't tell what day it was, nor could she ask Sarah about it until the swelling around her lips went down. How long ago had the accident happened? She merely existed, living in a world without communication. Day and night didn't exist, just her, God and pain. Somehow she continued to endure it.

Mattie dreamed of what she'd do when she got better. She could sell needlework to put a roof over her head. She wished she could touch the fine cloths she loved so much. Never again would she take her life for granted.

Before that fateful day when Cyrus sneaked into the canyon, she'd been lulled into complacency. There had been little contact with people other than the boys. She felt content to sit in her rocking chair on the porch with her needlework, enjoying her solitude. Years passed by without Mattie making much difference in anyone's life.

Never again would she hide the precious gifts God gave her. His purpose for giving gifts was to help others find His forgiveness. Mattie knew that now. She'd make every stitch count for something. With each tug on the needle, she'd say a prayer for the person who bought her work. She'd tell others about God's love for them and Christ's forgiveness for their sins. She would no longer sit and wait for nothing in particular. God was giving her a second chance to make a difference, and she'd use it wisely.

Many plans formulated in her mind during the times she was awake. Her heart overflowed with gratitude to God. She grew closer to Him than ever before. She'd never feel alone again.

The rain forming puddles of mud in the streets didn't bother Cyrus. He walked into the sheriff's office, leaving boot prints on the floor behind him.

"I came to see if you've heard anything from Mrs. Gordon."

"Not a thing. I've asked around, but nobody's seen her."

Cyrus sighed. "If you knew she was Will Gordon's mother, why didn't you apprehend them sooner?"

"I didn't know it was her until the day she came to visit that young feller she turned in as one of the Gordon gang members."

"Who'd she turn in?"

"Conrad Baker. It seems he was holding her prisoner. When a peddler showed up on their doorstep, she bought some things from him and wrapped up a note in the money. It said she was being held against her will by a member of the Will Gordon gang."

Cyrus chuckled. "She's got spunk."

"I didn't know who she was until that afternoon when she showed up at the jail, and Conrad called her Mother Gordon." The sheriff puffed on his cigar. "Beats anything I've ever seen."

"And you say nobody in town has seen her since that day."

Cyrus furrowed his brow. What was he missing? There's always a clue if he dug deep enough. "Where's Baker now? Maybe he might know something."

"We extradited him along with the rest of the rabble. They're all in Texas, awaiting trial, unless it's already taken place. I held him here, hoping for the gang to return. I sure would've liked to be the one to bring 'em all in." The sheriff leaned back in his chair. "I'd be famous by now."

"So, Will never made it back here?"

"Nope. For some reason they headed north a couple hours from here. I still think someone tipped 'em off."

"Conrad never got out of jail?"

"Nope. He stayed right here until the rest of the gang was caught by them rangers."

"Thanks, sheriff. You just gave me a clue as to where to find Mattie Gordon." Cyrus pulled his hat on and rushed out of the office.

"Aren't you gonna stay and tell me what clue I gave…?" he heard the sheriff call after him.

The single set of tracks meeting up with the gang. They weren't made by Conrad, like he'd originally thought. Cyrus groaned. He'd been only an hour from Mattie and left to go to Texas. By tracing their trail before they got caught, he'd find Mattie. Unfortunately, the rain would have washed out their tracks, but by now the whole territory knew of the capture. Surely someone noticed a woman with them and could tell him where she went.

Thank you, Lord. That quiet life on a farm with Mattie is starting to look like it might come true.

Cyrus left town feeling lighter than he had since that night in the cabin when he'd asked her if he could kiss her.

He rode slowly so he wouldn't miss the spot where the gang had turned north. Questions kept running through his mind. Will left Conrad behind to guard Mattie. Had they been keeping her prisoner the whole four months since he escaped from the canyon? Why had she gone out to warn them, when she'd already turned one of them in to the law? What was Will's reaction? Why had she gone with them? Was she there during the shootout? Cyrus knew the Texas Rangers caught up with the gang only a couple hours beyond the place where he left them.

He rode hard. Around noon, he reached the spot where the gang turned away from Scott City. Spurring his horse northward, excitement surged through his veins. He'd soon know where Mattie was.

Chapter Thirteen

There were no tracks for Cyrus to follow. The rain had washed them away. He headed for the town near the spot the newspapers reported the Gordon gang had been captured. Riding slowly through the slippery mud, he soon came upon an eerie sight.

A dead horse lay in the middle of the prairie. Losing one's horse while riding out in the middle of nowhere caused many deaths. Cyrus stopped for a closer look. Buzzards had done their job well. He shook his head and continued snooping around the area for further clues. The horse's right front leg was broken. Both rider and horse would have gone down together if they were galloping. The rider would definitely have been hurt.

All personal belongings were gone, including the saddle. Something flashed on the ground on the other side of the horse. He dismounted and walked over to pick it up. It was a small, silver hair comb, the one Mattie wore back at the canyon. His heart jumped and his arm froze a moment before reaching to pick up the precious object. He swallowed the lump in his throat and stuffed the comb into his pocket.

Lord, it's me again. I don't know what happened to Mattie, but You know where she is, so please lead me to her. She may need help.

After mounting, he headed toward the small town of Gove. Cyrus rode about another hour, and upon his arrival, he went straight to the sheriff's office.

"What can I do fer you?" The tall, lean man stood when Cyrus entered the small room.

"I'm looking for Mattie Gordon. She rode with the Gordon gang the day they were brought in."

The thin sheriff frowned. "Are you saying the gang had a woman?" He shook his head. "Weren't no woman with 'em when they were brought in."

"It's possible she wasn't with them when the rangers brought Will Gordon in. Have you heard of a woman in her forties being brought into town, maybe hurt from an accident?"

"Nope. I know everything that goes on in these parts, and I'm tellin' you, there weren't no woman with the Gordon gang."

Cyrus sighed. He thanked the man and walked out into the rain, pacing the street until he saw a shingle over a door that read, *Dr. Summler, Upstairs.* Entering the building, he took the steps two at a time. The second door on the left had white lettering on it, telling him this was the doctor's office.

The door was locked. Cyrus knocked several times, then sat down in the hallway and leaned against the wall. The man would have to return sometime to get supplies and record patient status. He'd wait. There was nothing else to do. Nowhere to go to look for Mattie, except the undertaker.

Lord, please don't take me there. Let Mattie be alive.

"Sir." Cyrus felt someone jiggling his shoulder.

He opened his eyes and jumped up.

"Sorry to startle you. Were you waiting for me?"

Cyrus blinked at the friendly face before him. "Are you Doc Summler?"

"That's me." The doctor inserted his key into the lock and opened the door. "Come in."

Cyrus followed him into the room and closed the door behind him.

"What can I do for you? Are you ill?" The doctor opened his medical bag and proceeded to extract various bottles of liquids and pills and set them gingerly on the rolltop-desk in the corner of the room.

"I'm fine," Cyrus answered. "I'm looking for Mattie Gordon. She's in her forties, about five foot three, dark blond hair, pretty, blue eyes."

"Hm." The doctor scratched his chin. "What makes you think I would know this lady? Has she some sort of ailment?"

Cyrus shook his head. "She's the outlaw, Will Gordon's, mother. She was riding with them the day the gang was apprehended. I have reason to believe her horse went down. I think she may have been hurt in the fall."

The doctor proceeded to put his medicines away in a glass-front cabinet, but his eyes narrowed almost imperceptibly. Perhaps in surprise, or realization.

"And are you related to the Gordon gang, too?" The doctor's keen eyes looked Cyrus over.

"No. I'm a bou—farmer. I met Mrs. Gordon about six months ago, and I'm looking for her."

"You don't look like a farmer. You look more like you could be a bounty hunter. Is that what you want with this woman?"

"No." Cyrus couldn't remember the last time someone got him flustered. "You see, I…" He'd never said it out loud before. This would be a good time to start. "I love her," he blurted out. "I want to marry her and retire to a farm somewhere."

The doctor's eyes squinted when he smiled, revealing many tiny lines around his eyes. "There, that wasn't so hard, was it?"

Cyrus let out deep sigh.

"I know where this lady of yours is."

Cyrus' breaths came in quick spurts. "Where is she? Is she alive? Can I see her?"

Dr. Summler put his coat back on and motioned for Cyrus to follow him. "She's staying at my sister's house. I'll fill you in on her injuries on the way there. I'm glad you're here. Until now, we didn't know who she was."

Cyrus followed the man to his buggy. Why hadn't she told anyone who she was? At least she was alive. Finally, after several months of separation, he would see Mattie. He shivered with excitement.

Cyrus braced himself for what he'd find when he saw her for the first time. His heart broke over hearing about her injuries. Once the swelling in her face went down, she would be able to move her lips and talk through clenched teeth. He could only imagine the world she been forced to live in.

When they arrived at a pretty, blue cottage outside of town, Dr. Summler introduced his sister, Sarah, to Cyrus. He followed her into a bedroom at the back of the house. The sunlight filtered through filmy white curtains, lighting up yellow walls. Mattie would love this room.

Lying quietly on the bed was a figure, most of her face wrapped in white gauze. Long strands of dark blond hair cushioned her neck. Mattie. Cyrus' chest tightened at the sight of her bruised and swollen lips. The left half of her face peeked out from the stark white wrapping.

His poor Mattie. The doctor nudged him farther into the room, and he went to the bedside. Sarah motioned for him to sit, so Cyrus took the chair beside the bed.

The doctor laid his hand on the invalid's left shoulder. "Are you Mattie Gordon?"

She nodded her head slightly, and Cyrus's heart leapt into his throat. How could this happen to someone as sweet and caring as Mattie? She lost her only son. Did she have to endure this too? A dull ache welled up inside of him, nearly taking his breath away. This was his fault. He should never have allowed himself to become involved with an outlaw's kin. He wished he could trade places with her to show her how sorry he was for all her pain.

Mattie's heart pounded inside her chest. They knew who she was. Someone must have come looking for her. Will?

"Mrs. Gordon," Dr. Summler said. "There's someone here to see you."

The doctor's hand on her shoulder was replaced with another one. This one seemed uncertain, yet somehow tenderer than doc's. Her heart sank into her belly. It couldn't be Will. The last time she saw him, he'd slapped her. She nearly choked on her tears.

"Mattie," the gentle, masculine voice spoke softly.

Cyrus. She forced her eye to open, and through blurred vision, she saw him leaning over her. She wanted to cry, but knew it would hurt too much, so she pushed the emotions back down into the recesses of her being.

"Mattie," he spoke in a near whisper, close to her ear. "I'm so sorry this happened. If I hadn't wanted one more bounty before I retired... She heard a sob escape his lips.

If he hadn't gone after Will, he would never have met her. Is that what he was saying? That he wished they hadn't met? That she turned out to be more trouble than he wanted in his life?

"If I could turn back time, I wouldn't have stayed there in Hays waiting for Will. But I had to find you. I needed to find you."

Mattie wanted to yell at him. He wasn't making any sense. Waiting for Will in Hays? Sorry he was looking for the bounty?

Was he with the posse that day? No. Her heart pounded in her chest. He didn't love her. *Please, Lord. Make him go away.*

Cyrus squeezed her shoulder. "I know you can't talk yet, but you will very soon."

Mattie had to know about Will. Though her jaw was bound tight and her lips and face swollen, she had so many questions.

"Will." The muffled sound emanating from her lips didn't sound like English.

"What was that?" he asked. "Did you say, 'Will'?"

She nodded her head.

"No one knew who you were, so you probably didn't hear any of the details. Will put up a fight and was shot in the leg, but he's fine. Four others were wounded and three are dead. Jake Bord, Carl Bledsoe and Tully O'Toole."

Her heart broke for the men she'd treated as her own sons. Cyrus remained quiet for a while, and Mattie was grateful to him for allowing her this time to grieve.

Then he leaned toward her. "I got your telegraph about a witness that would prove Will's innocence." His voice came from somewhere close to her head. "Would this have something to do with Conrad?"

She nodded her head.

"I don't know what's going on with the trial right now. I'll send a telegram to Sheriff Wilson. He'll see to it that Will's lawyer gets the notice."

Mattie wanted to be there in person to help her son, but that would be impossible now. Dare she ask Cyrus for help? He'd been on the trail a long time and might want to go back to Texas. "Go help Will." The words spoken through her clenched jaw and swollen mouth probably didn't sound right.

Cyrus didn't respond. Perhaps he didn't understand her.

"Go…Texas… please."

Mattie heard footsteps in the room. "Mrs. Gordon needs to rest now," the doctor said.

"If that's what you want me to do, then I'll go to Texas rather than send a telegram." Cyrus' voice held resolve. "But you have to promise me you'll do everything the doctor orders so that we can have a nice, long talk when I get back."

She nodded, then felt something on her cheek. Had Cyrus kissed her? This man confused her.

"God bless you, Mattie Gordon," Cyrus said from the other side of the room. "You've affected my life in ways you'll never know."

Then she heard footsteps leaving the room and a door shutting. The doctor began fussing with her bandages and took her temperature and pulse.

Perhaps Cyrus did care about her more than she thought, but she was too tired to hold the thought and gave in to sleep.

Cyrus left the little cottage in the country, emotions surging through his mind. Seeing Mattie this way tugged at his heart. He knew she loved her son very much. To ask Cyrus to help her could only mean one thing. She trusted him. And if she trusted him, could she one day love him as he loved her?

He headed to town to get a trail pack together before leaving for Texas.

The rain let up after a day of riding. Grateful to see the sun again, Cyrus packed his rain poncho and mounted the horse. Even Shadow seemed happy to see the sun, and they made good time the next day.

Cyrus had no idea what he'd do once he got to Texas. All he knew was that Conrad had information that could get the murder charges against Will dropped. Should he talk to Conrad first, or Will's lawyer? How would he approach the outlaw? The gang knew he was the one ultimately responsible for landing them in jail. Would any of them speak with him?

Cyrus shook his head. This wouldn't be easy. He squared his shoulders. How many other men in the world did difficult things for the love of a good woman? He doubted many had, for the love he felt for Mattie was unlike anything anyone could have experienced. The thought of her made him smile. Yet her hurt and helplessness pained him.

Stop it. This is too much analyzing for one man.

The next week, he tried not to think so much. Just get to Texas and do what he could. It would be up to God to work out all the details. This kind of trust was new to Cyrus, but the past six months had been full of different things he never thought would happen to him.

He rode into Abilene and headed straight for the jail. "I'm here to see Conrad Baker," he told the deputy behind the front desk. "Privately," he added.

"That's going to be pretty hard to do, since he's sharing the cell with another man."

"What would it take to see him in a separate room?"

"Mr., unless you're a lawyer, which you don't look much like one, that ain't going to happen."

Cyrus thought a moment. "What's his lawyer's name and where can I find him?"

"His lawyer is Barry Ellson." The deputy spat into the nearby spittoon. "You'll probably find him over at the courthouse."

"Thanks." Cyrus passed the courthouse earlier, so he knew where to go.

Inside the huge brick building, a maze of hallways, staircases and waiting areas jutted from a large main lobby. He headed for a pretty, young lady sitting behind a mahogany desk on the far left side of the hall.

"May I help you, sir?" The lady's smile was contagious and Cyrus returned it with one of his own.

"I'm looking for a lawyer named Ellson."

"Mr. Ellson is in the building, but he's in court now. You're welcome to wait for him over there." She pointed to a group of benches and chairs.

"Do you have any idea how long that will take?"

"I'm sorry, sir, but I don't know. It could be a few minutes, or it might take hours."

Cyrus sighed. More waiting.

"I'll be glad to tell him who's calling on him when he comes downstairs."

"I don't think that will do any good, because we've never met before."

"You may want to go to his office on the corner of Second and Pine. He has associates there who might be able to help you."

"Oh, I'm not in need of a lawyer. I need to talk to him as soon as possible about one of his present clients, Conrad Baker."

"You're welcome to wait here for him. If you need to leave, I can deliver a message to him when he comes down."

"Thanks, miss. My name's Cyrus Braydon."

She wrote his name on a tablet, followed by a brief note.

Cyrus shrugged and went to the area designated for waiting. He took up a newspaper. It contained updates about the Gordon gang capture. On the second page he found a short article mentioning his name as being instrumental in their capture. Authorities were looking for Cyrus in order to give him the reward money. The author of the article said to the best of his knowledge, no bounty hunter had ever walked away from a payment before. He touted Cyrus as some sort of frontier hero.

Cyrus tossed the paper aside. Him? A hero? He wasn't trying to be a champion, nor was he trying to capture Will Gordon. His main goal had been to find Mattie again. Now he was in Texas, a thousand miles from the woman he wanted to marry, trying to get murder charges dropped for a notorious man with a bounty on his head. And he could trace the start of this confusion back to the day he met Mattie Gordon.

Cyrus stood and paced the room. Maybe he'd wait until this whole ordeal was over before he claimed the money. On one hand, it would give him his little piece of heaven he'd been dreaming about. He'd need it if he were to marry. Then again, it might cause Mattie to turn away from him. All this thinking gave him a headache.

He sat again and tried reading more of the paper. Finally he resorted to staring out the window at the throng of people in the street below. He watched people walk up and down the boardwalks. Ladies and gentlemen walked arm in arm, smiling and talking. How nice it would be to have Mattie on his arm.

"Ahem...Mr. Braydon?"

Cyrus spun around and saw a short, rotund man with white hair, extending his hand toward him. Cyrus shook his hand.

"Yes, sir."

"I'm Barry Ellson." The man looked up at Cyrus over his small glasses. You're looking for me regarding one of my clients?"

"Yes. I need to talk to you about Conrad Baker."

The man's eyes narrowed. "What kind of business?"

"I have reason to believe Conrad has information regarding a witness to the murder Will Gordon is being charged with. This witness can testify that Gordon is innocent of the charges."

The man took a white handkerchief out of his pocket and wiped his forehead with it, then tucked it away. "Perhaps we'd better talk. Come with me to my office. We'll continue this discussion there."

Mr. Ellson walked with purpose toward his office and Cyrus followed him. They didn't speak for four blocks. Arriving at the office building, Mr. Ellson unlocked his door. He motioned for Cyrus to enter and sit down. Then he closed the door behind him, walked around the desk and sat in his chair.

"Now, tell me more about this, please."

Cyrus spent the next fifteen minutes telling him about Mattie and showed him her telegram. He finished by explaining how she conveyed the message that Conrad knew something about the murder.

"Will Gordon's trial is set to begin in two days." The man rubbed his chin. "I'll look into the situation and get back with you. I can't promise you he'll talk, nor can I say whether his testimony will do any good. But I'll see what I can do."

Cyrus exhaled in relief. That was all he could expect.

"Where are you staying?"

"I haven't got a room yet. I've been traveling a lot recently, so I don't have a lot of money right now."

"Head on down Second Street to Mulberry. Turn right and go down about four blocks. Turn left on Sixth and go to the second house on the left. Tell Mrs. Jodston I sent you, and she'll give you a good rate for a small room and good food."

Cyrus stood and extended his hand to the lawyer. "Thanks. I appreciate it."

"Don't mention it. I'll get in touch with you when I know something. Good afternoon, Mr. Braydon."

Cyrus shoved his hat down onto his head and walked out of the building with a strange, unexplainable feeling he shouldn't trust that lawyer. He did the best he could, but something didn't sit right with him. He prayed for everything to go smoothly in Will's defense. All he wanted was for Mattie to be happy and know he did all he could to help her boy.

Mrs. Jodston was the friendliest boarding house owner Cyrus ever met. She immediately filled him up on roasted chicken, potatoes, corn, buttermilk biscuits and gravy. He ate every morsel of the delicious food.

After supper, Mr. Ellison arrived, and he and Cyrus went outside to talk.

"Conrad says he doesn't know what you're talking about. He never heard of you, and you should mind your own business."

"Did you cut him a deal if he'd talk? Maybe get him a lighter sentence for keeping an innocent man from being hung and helping to catch the real murderer?"

Mr. Ellison shifted his eyes, looking everywhere but straight at Cyrus. "He said he'd have loved a lighter sentence, but he truly didn't know anything about that murder."

Cyrus thanked the man and watched him walk down the street. It didn't make any sense that Conrad wouldn't take an offer of a lighter sentence. Now that Will was also in jail, Conrad's fear of him should disappear. In fact, if Conrad could get Will's sentence reduced, Cyrus figured Will would be mighty happy about that and would thank Conrad. Things didn't look right in Abilene that night.

Cyrus promised Mattie to do everything he could, so he headed straight for the jail and asked to see Conrad. The sheriff led him to the cell where Conrad and another gang member sat on bunks with an old crate between them, playing a game of cards.

They both looked up when Cyrus entered.

"Baker," the sheriff said. "You got a visitor." Then he left.

"What do you want?" Conrad barely looked in Cyrus' direction.

"I was sent by Mattie Gordon to talk to you."

"Yeah? Well I don't have anything to say to you."

"You don't have to talk to me. I'm just disappointed in you. I thought you were smarter than you showed today when your lawyer offered you a deal that might lighten your sentence." He shook his head. The outlaw stood and walked toward the bars.

"What deal?"

"The one Mr. Ellison offered you today in exchange for your testimony."

"That two-bit lawyer never came here today."

Cyrus suspected that was the case. And he could be certain Will's lawyer was bought off too. But by whom?

"Listen. Mattie has been treating you fellas like you were her own boys. You owe it to her to help Will any way you can. She had an accident and couldn't talk, but she led me to believe you know something about a witness to the murder Will is being charged with."

"Mother Gordon is hurt? Will she be all right?"

"Yeah. She'll make it. But all she ever wanted for you boys was to not get killed through all this."

The young man shifted his weight onto his other foot. "So, what's this deal you were talking about?"

He didn't deny it. Conrad definitely knows something. But the only way his testimony would be heard in Will's trial is if one of the attorneys brought it up. And Cyrus was certain neither lawyer could be trusted.

"You'll hear the deal soon enough."

Cyrus left the man to stare at the back of his head. He didn't know that much about how the justice system worked, but he knew someone who did. Cyrus sighed and headed to the telegraph office before it closed.

Chapter Fourteen

Sarah read aloud every day. Mattie liked that she never ran out of things to comment on or talk about, even though the conversation went only one way. Until then, Mattie hadn't realized how much she'd missed the company of another woman. She wished Cyrus would love her and ask her to marry him. Then they could settle down on a ranch somewhere, and she would enjoy getting to know her neighbors.

"Say, Mrs. Gordon," Sarah suddenly said. "Wasn't the man who came to see you named Cyrus Braydon?"

Mattie nodded her head.

"There's a story about him in the newspaper. Let's see. I'll start here... 'Although a group of Texas Rangers actually captured the notorious Will Gordon and his gang of outlaws, they credit their success to the bounty hunter, Cyrus Braydon. Mr. Braydon tracked down the desperados, then alerted Texas authorities of the gang's whereabouts. The rangers say Mr. Braydon left them when they were little more than an hour from catching up to the gang. They agreed the reward money should go to Mr. Braydon.

He did all the work and was able to accomplish what many lawmen and other bounty hunters have been trying to do for several years. With the Will Gordon gang going to trial soon, local authorities hope Mr. Braydon will step up and claim his reward money.'"

Mattie couldn't believe it. She'd thought Cyrus wasn't going after Will. Sheriff Wilson told her Cyrus had given up bounty hunting. Yet he was there that day, leading the Texas Rangers right to Will. She felt like throwing something across the room. She'd been wrong. The man she fell in love with was not only a bounty hunter, but also a liar and a coward. Hadn't he called for the rangers to help him, then turned and run away?

She'd been a fool to trust him. He probably didn't even go to Abilene. He probably laughed all the way home to Waco. Why did he come visit her in the first place?

When he told her he accepted the Lord into his heart, was that a lie too? Had he only told her that because he thought that was what she wanted to hear?

Mattie changed her mind about what she wanted the future to be like. Maybe she'd go back to the canyon and live there forever, away from the things of man. None of them could be trusted. Especially bounty hunters.

A loud, crashing sound interrupted Mattie's sleep.

"I'm sorry, I dropped my bag," Dr. Summler said. "Were you sleeping?"

She nodded.

"It's time to remove your bandages and allow some fresh air to help heal your wounds the rest of the way. You'll still have your jaw bound up for a few more weeks, but it looks like the swelling has gone down quite a bit. That means you'll be able to talk better."

Mattie's heart pounded with excitement. She felt the doctor touch the side of her head and then the snip, snip of scissors.

"I don't want you to move your head until I can bind your jaw back up."

She responded by lying still.

He continued cutting the bandages that held Mattie prisoner for what seemed like a month to her. As he peeled the layers away, the summer air felt cool on her head.

The doctor removed the pieces of gauze still covering her eyes. "Now, open your eyes slowly."

She did as he asked and the light in the room beamed brightly. Closing her eyes and putting her hand over them, she winced from the pain.

"It's all right. You have some scars and bruises that still need to heal, but they're coming along nicely. Now let me shade your eyes and you try opening them again."

This time the light wasn't quite so blinding, and soon Mattie was able to focus on objects in the room. She looked into the kind face of the doctor. He looked like he might be a few years older than her.

The doctor worked quickly to get her jaw bound so she couldn't move it.

"My eyes won't open all the way," she said through clenched teeth.

"They're still swollen. You scratched your face pretty bad." He leaned very close to examine her eyes with a magnifying glass. She felt his warm breath on her cheek. "They look much better than I expected. I'd say you're pretty lucky."

Lucky? No. It was God. He'd answered her prayers for a speedy recovery. "How long have I been here?"

"About two weeks."

It felt longer than that.

Sarah entered the room and took Mattie's hand. "It's good to see you getting better. You're a pretty lady. It's no wonder your Mr. Braydon looked so sad to see you hurt."

He's not my Mr. Braydon.

"He cried when you nodded your head that you were Mattie Gordon."

What a confusing man. Would she ever be able to figure him out? Did she want to? She sighed. *Yes.* Despite everything, she couldn't stop loving him.

The doctor continued to examine her cuts and applied a salve while Mattie prayed silently.

Lord, please take this love away from me if it's not in Your will for my life. Ever since that day he held a gun to my head on the porch, I knew my life was in for some changes. But I only want the changes You desire for me. I give Cyrus into Your hands. Amen.

She expected to not feel anything for Cyrus, but she did. Her life had never been so perplexing.

The following days brought physical healing for Mattie. The doctor exclaimed over her progress, calling it a miracle. Mattie knew God chose to heal her quickly.

She and Sarah became friends. They talked until Mattie's jaw got sore, and then Sarah would read to her from the Bible or from the newspaper. As Will's trial progressed, the news stories became shorter. It seemed the reporters were tiring of this story and went on to find new and more exciting news.

Then one day Sarah read how the judge excused himself from serving in Will's trial, which would continue as soon as the governor appointed a new judge. Mattie didn't know what to think. She didn't understand legal affairs. She wished she could be there to support her son. Why hadn't Conrad testified? Cyrus evidently failed her. He probably wasn't anywhere near Abilene. Maybe he claimed the reward money, bought a small ranch and was sitting on the porch watching the same sunset she did each night.

How could she love a man who made her so angry? She'd

have to figure out a way to go to Texas and tell them what Conrad told her. Mattie would make them listen to her.

Cyrus yawned and stretched. He was becoming lazy from sitting around the courthouse for the past several weeks. But today he didn't need to go there. The governor was coming to personally see that Will got a fair trial.

It amazed Cyrus to discover the judge wasn't willing to listen to the new lawyer he'd secured for Conrad when he tried to tell him of Conrad's new evidence. That was when Cyrus became furious and sent a telegram to the governor himself.

He didn't know if it would do any good, or if the governor would even get the telegram. But the reply came in time to thwart the efforts of those who wanted to see Will hang for the murder of a banker's wife. The governor ordered the judge to step down and the proceedings to be suspended, pending an investigation into allegations of wrongdoing.

His thoughts turned toward Mattie. He knew she'd be pleased to know he'd managed to get the trial stopped. He wanted to get on his horse and ride north until he found himself in her arms, and never let her out of his sight again. But it was important for him to stay where he was. The governor might want to talk to him about all he'd seen and heard relating to the trial.

He decided to send Mattie a telegram.

Mattie had enough of being an invalid. Two more weeks of waiting for her jaw to heal. How could she endure it? She'd lost weight from the bowls full of broth she'd been limited to eating. When she put on her dress, it hung from her shoulders like a potato sack. Her first day of eating real food became a milestone in her healing process, even though the doctor limited what she could eat.

Against his advice, she packed her belongings and left Sarah's house. She'd been keeping up with the trial, what little news there'd been about Will. The only thing she could think to do was go to Texas to see how she could help him.

After leaving a note and some money for the doctor, Mattie didn't have much money left, but she knew where she could get more. She purchased a stagecoach ticket to Springfield, Colorado. From there, she'd rent a conveyance to return to the canyon.

In town, Mattie noticed stares from passers-by. She knew some of her cuts weren't quite healed yet, but she figured that wasn't the reason for their gawking. By now the whole county knew a notorious outlaw gang had been arrested in this town. She lifted her head and walked down the street. What counted most was that she had God in her heart.

She knew she'd live the rest of her life as an unmarried widow. After gathering her furniture from the cabin when Will's trial was over, she'd move to the town closest to the prison. She'd get a small place and live out her days, doing needlework for money and visiting her son whenever she could.

Meanwhile, she'd testify of God's love to anyone who'd listen. Mattie would never again hide away in a canyon.

The stagecoach bounced along the rutted road, swirling dirt through the air. Mattie hated these contraptions. But at least she didn't become as bone-weary as when traveling by horseback. In order to keep the dust to a minimum, the passengers closed the window flaps. It became so stuffy inside the coach, they had to open them back up, and the dust choked them again.

The only bright spot in the trip was when they stopped to rest the horses or transfer passengers. Mattie took advantage of the rest periods by walking the kinks out of her sore body.

Throughout the trip to Springfield, Mattie prayed constantly. Each day her heart healed a bit more, and she began to speak to others on the stage with more confidence. Amazingly, they responded to her with gentle answers.

Stepping out of the coach in Springfield, she breathed deeply of the fresh Colorado air. She loved this place. Although she recognized familiar faces, she never made any friends. If she had, would they have turned Will in long ago? The thought caused a knot in her stomach. The realization that her own solitude perpetuated her son's lawbreaking escapades hurt her. How blind she'd been. The life she thought so relaxing and rewarding was nothing more than that of a caged animal.

Thank you, Lord, for taking me out of there and showing me how to really live.

Mattie held her head high as she walked the streets she'd visited once a year to shop for supplies. At the livery, she rented a horse and surrey, then parked it in front of the mercantile. Upon entering the shop, several heads turned her direction. Some stared openly at her, while others quickly looked away. People who knew her and had done business with her before now acted as though she were the strangest of strangers. She gathered a few provisions and took them up to the front counter.

"How are you doing, Mrs. Talone?"

"I'm doing well. It looks like you've had some sort of accident. Are you okay?"

"Yes. It was pretty bad, but I've been healing nicely."

"I'm so sorry about your accident, but it looks like you're going to be fine." The lady smiled, which warmed Mattie's heart.

Mattie smiled back at her. Mrs. Talone didn't know how true her statement was. "Yes, I'll be fine. This will probably be the last time I ever see you, so I wish you a good life filled with the Lord's blessings."

Mrs. Talone looked surprised. "Thank you, Mrs. …I don't think I ever knew your name."

"Mattie Gordon." Mattie reached out to shake the woman's hand.

She took it, then her eyes grew round as saucers. "Mattie Gordon? The mother of that outlaw they're trying down in Texas?"

Mattie cringed inwardly. "That's me."

The woman's mouth nearly came unhinged as it dropped open. Someone gasped behind her, and she heard the door open and close.

"That's about the same reaction I had when I found out my son was a notorious outlaw." Mattie fished through her handbag and pulled out the little money she had left. "He fooled me into thinking he worked for a huge outfit in Oklahoma. I'm glad someone finally found him." She lowered her gaze. That someone had put her son in jail and stole her heart while doing it. *Stop*. She had to move on. Forget Cyrus. Focus on Will. "How much do I owe you?"

"That'll be four twenty-five."

Mattie paid her bill and left the mercantile. Several people milled about, and quickly gathered around her.

"We don't want the likes of you around here."

"Get out of our town."

"Don't ever show your face in Springfield again."

Someone pushed her out into the street, the crowd shouting terrible insults around her. A wad of mud hit the side of her face, causing her to loose her footing. The sting on her face wasn't nearly as deep as the one in her heart.

Mattie scrambled to her feet and pushed through the throng toward the rented buggy. A large hand took hold of her arm and she felt herself being pulled along the street.

"Go back about your business, everyone," a deep voice shouted beside her. "Go on! Git!"

The people slowly dispersed, and Mattie looked up into the eyes of her rescuer. He wasn't looking at her, but glowered at those around him. She saw the tin badge on his chest and sighed in relief.

The sheriff escorted her to the jailhouse and offered her a seat inside. "News travels fast in these parts, Mrs. Gordon. I'm sorry about that mob in the street. People can be pretty narrow-minded sometimes."

"Thank you, sheriff. I appreciate your help." She reached up to her face and touched the spot where the mud hit her.

The sheriff reached into his pocket and produced a red handkerchief and handed it to her.

"Thank you again." She took the cloth and wiped her face.

"Ma'am, I've seen you around here a few times before. I never would have thought you were an outlaw's mother."

"Sheriff, am I being held for a reason?"

"No. I'm not holding you. I wanted to warn you."

"Warn me about what?"

"Nobody knows where you've been living all these years. They've seen you come into town and lay up enough supplies to feed a small army." He leaned forward. "They say you were hiding the Will Gordon gang."

Mattie swallowed hard. Hiding them? "Sir, I took care of my son and his men. But I didn't know they were outlaws until a bounty hunter showed up on my doorstep about six months ago."

He nodded. "I understand. But I think it would be best if you move out of this area right away. Now that people know the famous outlaw gang lived around these parts, they won't let you rest. They'll want souvenirs. Some are already saying there might be money hidden around the place."

The significance of what he said hit her like a bolt of lightening. Will was in jail, yet she was still in possible danger. "There's something I want to get from home first, then I planned to head down to Texas to be near my son."

"That's the smart thing to do."

"But I rented the surrey overnight. I'll have to bring it back into town."

"Hmmm." He scratched his chin. "You shouldn't come back here. You could leave it at your house and I could go by and pick it up tomorrow. Would that help you?"

"I had planned on taking the stage to Texas, so I'll bring it back before I board tomorrow." Mattie needed to get to Will before the trial was over. She hadn't seen anything in the newspapers about Conrad being a witness in his murder trial. She didn't have time for games.

"I'll bet you everything I got that you're going to be followed home today. No. I think you better hop on the afternoon stage today and be rid of this town."

How could Mattie convey to him about her stash of money? She needed it to buy her stage ticket. She knew it was money Will got from his unscrupulous dealings. He'd given it to her throughout the years, and she'd saved it for whenever she needed it. That time was now.

"There's something I need to get from home, sheriff. I can't leave town without it."

"How far is your place from here?"

"Fifteen miles or so. Why?"

"I could escort you out there and we would be back in town by supper time."

She sighed. If that's what it would take, she'd agree. Mattie nodded.

"Fine. Let's go."

They exited the jailhouse together. The crowd in the street had grown. The sheriff helped her into the buggy, mounted his horse, and rode beside her out of town. The citizens must have understood the meaning. Nobody followed them to the canyon. Leastwise, Mattie hoped they hadn't.

Not wanting the sheriff to know what she was looking for,

Mattie went to the house first and looked around for something she could take with her. She had already taken all her smaller household items to Scott City. Only a couple pieces of furniture remained here. Let those vultures back in town have it if that's all they care about. There simply wasn't anything she could do. The lawman could think what he wanted. She needed to get her money and head to Texas.

Mattie exited the house and walked past the sheriff. She could feel him watching her, but he remained silent.

In the outhouse she locked the door behind her. Standing on the platform beside the hole, she reached up into the walls, pulling a metal file out from between one of the boards. She used the file to pry up a loose board on the seat. Nailed to the underside was a flour sack. Ripping the sack off the nail, Mattie pulled the money out. Putting the board back into place, she then tossed the sack and the file into the hole and stuffed the money into her secret pouch in her garter.

She took a moment to think and pray. Will got this money from innocent citizens. But she needed it now to get to him. When she got to Texas, she'd give whatever was left to the proper authorities.

Please forgive me if this is wrong, Lord. You know my heart. All I want is for Will to get acquitted of the murder charges and to find Your forgiveness.

When she pushed the door open, the sunlight beamed into the tiny structure. She squinted against it, allowing her eyes to adjust to the brightness. Staring at the house for the last time, her thoughts turned toward Cyrus. She remembered the day he asked her for a kiss, and now she wished she'd have accepted it. But would he still care for her when he saw her again?

Now that she was finally on her way to Texas, she wondered if their paths would cross again. She shook off the thoughts, but couldn't easily rid her heart of the love she felt for him. All she could do was give everything in her heart to God to work it all out for her good. She believed He would.

"Mrs. Gordon?"

Mattie jumped and drew in a breath.

"Is everything all right?"

"Yes. Everything is as fine as it can be, under the circumstances." She didn't know what to expect. Would Will have already been exonerated from the murder charge? Or sent to the gallows? How would Cyrus react when he saw her again? She couldn't bear to lose either of them, but she wouldn't know anything until she got to Texas.

Chapter Fifteen

It had been too long since Cyrus sent Mattie the telegram telling her of Will's new trial. Worry had wracked his mind until he couldn't stand not hearing from her any longer, so he'd ridden to Scott City to make sure she was okay. Cyrus dismounted and ground tied his horse, a trick he'd learned many years before. By leaving the reins hanging straight down, the animal thinks he is tied to the ground and won't go anywhere.

He stepped up onto the porch of the pretty, white cottage and knocked on the door. When the trial was finally over and he returned to his little farmhouse, he'd paint it white. Today, he'd ask Mattie to marry him. All his dreams would be realized. The thought made him smile.

"Mr. Braydon. What a surprise." Sarah opened the door wide, smiling at him. "Please, come in."

Cyrus took his hat off and entered the house.

"I didn't expect to see you again, not after I sent you that telegram," Sarah told him.

"Telegram? I didn't get a telegram."

"Oh, Dear." Sarah wrung her hands. "I'd hoped to prevent this sort of thing."

"Is something wrong? Is Mattie okay?" Dread crept into Cyrus' throat and threatened to choke him. He'd never forgive himself if something happened to her while he loitered around Abilene waiting for the new trial.

"Oh, Mrs. Gordon is fine. But she's not here."

"Not here? I don't understand." Had he heard her correctly?

"Would you like to sit down?" Sarah pointed to a chair.

"No, thank you. I won't be staying for a social visit. Where's Mattie?"

"She's gone."

"Gone where?"

"To Texas."

Cyrus moaned.

"Are you all right, Mr. Braydon?"

How did things keep getting mixed up? His heart nearly sank to his boots. He'd been ready to swoop Mattie up in his arms and carry her to a new life with him. Now he faced more time out on the trail. "When did she leave?"

"About two days ago."

He sighed. That was about the time he'd sent the telegram. He was certain of one thing, when he finally caught up to that feisty little lady, he wouldn't let her out of his sight again.

Cyrus rode hard for a week and entered Abilene tired, hungry and dirty. He'd done that sort of stretch before, but lately, it caught up to him in the form of sore joints and aching muscles.

After leaving his horse at the livery, he sought out a clean bath and a soft bed. Mrs. Jodson welcomed him back to her boarding house. She promptly took him upstairs to a room, and drew him a hot bath in the room down the hall.

After washing and dressing in fresh clothes, Cyrus headed out into the streets of Abilene to find Mattie. He checked all the hotels and boarding houses, but there was no sign of her. Impatient, he headed for the sheriff's office. Perhaps they'd seen her. The mother of the notorious Will Gordon would certainly draw attention.

The sheriff looked up when he entered the jailhouse. Recognition registered on his face. He nodded. "Afternoon, Braydon. Is there something I can do for you?"

"I was wondering if you've heard anything about Will Gordon's mother being in town?"

The sheriff's eyebrows shot up. "Well, now. I haven't heard about that. I'm sure it would cause quite a stir." He leaned forward. "Do you figure she'll be along soon? I never reckoned an outlaw like Gordon as ever having a mother." The man chuckled to himself.

"Yeah, I know what you mean. But this is one sweet little lady. She's about five feet tall, dark blond hair, blue eyes."

"Haven't seen nor heard of her bein' around these parts. But I'll keep my eyes out for her. Should I send her to find you if I do?"

"No. I'd appreciate if you'd leave word at Mrs. Jodson's if you hear anything."

"I'll do that."

Cyrus thanked him and stepped out into the hot afternoon sunshine. He looked down one side of the street, then the other. Settling on a bench in front of the post office near the middle of town, he scanned the throng of people for Mattie's pretty face.

The wait grew agonizing. Tiring of searching the crowd, he returned to the boarding house, hoping to hear news of Mattie. But there was none.

The next morning Cyrus decided to attend the trial and wait for Mattie there. He searched the room, but didn't see her. He worried all through the witnesses' testimonies. Apparently, while he was gone Conrad Baker had been subpoenaed to testify about his knowledge of the murder case, and the prosecution paraded witness after witness to the cattle rustling charges. The prosecution rested its case and the defense attorney worked diligently to refute the previous witnesses' testimonies. He wasn't doing a very good job. After all, he didn't have any witnesses himself, other than the gang members. Things didn't look good for Will Gordon.

If Mattie didn't arrive soon, she'd miss the entire proceedings. He prayed she was all right. She'd left two days before him, but wasn't here yet. It worried him. Lord, please take care of her.

The day wore on with tired, weary testimonies, occasional bantering between the attorneys and a yawning judge. Cyrus hated the slowness of the legal process. He craved being outdoors, and when the defense rested its case, relief filled him.

The judge instructed the jury in their duty to come to a fair and honest conclusion, weighing all the evidence and not interjecting their own opinions into the case. The members of the jury filed out of the courtroom through a back door. The rest of the people were dismissed.

Cyrus picked up his hat and turned to leave. Then he saw her. *Mattie!*

His gut clenched tight. It felt like someone laid a hard blow to his ribcage at the sight of her. The right side of her face bore scars from her accident, and her eyes revealed depth of sorrow over her son. He couldn't remember ever seeing someone so sad before. It tore through his heart. Their eyes met for a moment through the mob as everyone pushed forward to get outside.

A tear escaped down her cheek, and she brushed it away with a gloved finger. Then she turned and walked out the door amidst a sea of people.

"Mattie! Wait!" She acted as thought she hadn't heard his call, or maybe she ignored it. He pushed and shoved his way out of the courthouse, frantically looking for her. But she was nowhere in sight. She couldn't have been that far ahead of him.

Cyrus searched all possible places that rented rooms, but he couldn't find her. Then he looked in all the eating establishments, thinking she would get some supper. With sadness in his heart, he returned to Mrs. Jodson's place. The only thing he could do was wait for her on the courthouse steps in the morning.

Sleep eluded him. The remembrance of Mattie's distress left him hurting for her. He wanted to hold and comfort her. If only he could bring back her sweet smile. For the first time in his life, Cyrus understood what his chosen profession cost others. Bringing outlaws to justice was a good thing. But realizing how it tore families apart and caused deep sorrow was enough for him to know he'd never go after another bounty. Let someone else do the job. His heart had been torn between doing what was right and his love for Mattie, but he wrestled with the dilemma no longer. All that mattered to him now was Mattie.

Would she blame him the rest of her life for losing her son? Could she truly love him? The man who brought Will to justice? Even if they would marry and settle down on a farm somewhere, would part of her hold a grudge against him? He could only hope and pray she would love him back.

Tomorrow would bring him the answers to all his heart's questions. But was he ready to hear them?

Mattie lay on her bedroll beside her camp. Such a peaceful place. Babbling stream, rolling pastureland, a few scrub oaks by the banks. Despite the tranquil setting, she hadn't slept much. At seeing Cyrus again, her heart did flip-flops. She loved him. Certain he didn't feel the same about her, she was thrown into turmoil. It looked as if the trial didn't go favorably in Will's direction. Whatever the outcome, she wouldn't hold Cyrus responsible for it. Deep down, she knew this wasn't his fault.

Will was an outlaw. He hadn't committed that murder, but he'd made other poor decisions. Had Mattie become aware sooner, maybe she would have been able to talk him out of these crimes. Perhaps not. But she owed Cyrus a debt of gratitude for opening her eyes to the truth. She'd been living in a fog, unable to see things going on right under her nose. Or perhaps she refused to see it. Either way, because of Cyrus Braydon, Will would no longer pilfer honest people's hard-earned money. Will had to face his mistakes like a man.

She prayed all night long for her son. Prayed for the outcome of the trial, and to accept whatever that may be, absent of any remorse. She even prayed that Cyrus would be able to get on with his life. But he had been at the trial. He hadn't gone home to his farm outside of Waco like she thought he had.

She camped close enough to town that she could be there in less than ten minutes after the lawyer sent word to her. Mattie had no stomach for breakfast, so she rolled over on her side and read her Bible, waiting for news the jury had returned.

She remembered the scene from the day before. All the Gordon gang members, sitting at three crowded tables, their attorneys wearing expensive suits and sitting importantly beside them. Although she only saw the backs of their heads, Mattie knew each of them so well, she could have described the looks on each of their faces at that moment in time. All except for Will's. Would he be scowling, frowning, or would there be no expression at all?

She realized she knew so little about him and it saddened her. There were many things she would have done differently, had she known sooner. But all that was behind her. God forgave her ignorance. There wasn't anything she could do now, but pray for God's will.

Around noon, she ate a stale biscuit and an apple. Then she heard the sound of horse hooves speeding toward her. Her heart jumped into her throat. Dread seeped through every nerve in her body, and she felt a lump forming in her throat. She'd asked the lawyer representing Will to send word. This was the moment she'd wished would never come, yet had been waiting for.

"Mrs. Gordon!" a male voice called to her.

She watched him ride into her camp.

"The jury's made a decision. The judge is ruling in twenty minutes."

She nodded, her voice failing. Taking a deep breath, she headed back to Abilene.

Reaching the courthouse, Mattie didn't look into anyone's eyes, even though she felt people staring. Maybe it was the scars, or maybe they knew she was Will Gordon's mother. When she felt a warm hand on her arm, she turned.

Cyrus!

His eyes held a tenderness that made her want to cry. She wanted to fling herself against his chest and never leave his comforting grip. But she reminded herself he didn't love her. He'd only been after the reward money the whole time. If he needed this gesture as a way to ease his own conscience, then so be it.

She allowed him to guide her into the courtroom, then scooted into a bench. Cyrus sat beside her. People packed the room like peas in a canning jar. Elbow to elbow, Mattie became acutely aware of Cyrus' presence beside her. She was grateful he hadn't said anything. Nothing would have been appropriate.

A moment later, a side door opened and a dozen armed deputies walked through, escorting their prisoners who filed into the room one by one.

Mattie's heart warmed when she saw her son enter, head lowered, eyes averted to the floor. She thought she saw penitence there, and it gave her hope.

Single file, the members of the jury walked in and took their chairs.

The bailiff entered the room. "All rise."

Everyone in the room rose. The judge entered and sat behind the huge desk.

"Everyone, please be seated."

The judge banged his gavel. "This court is now in session." He turned to the jury. "Members of the jury, have you reached a verdict?"

One man stood to his feet. "Yes, Your Honor. We have."

The judge nodded. "You may read the verdict."

"We, the members of the jury, find the defendant, Will Gordon, not guilty of murder."

Thank you, Lord. Mattie's heart soared within her.

An outcry among the people caused the judge to pound his gavel. "There will be order in the court!"

The people quieted again.

"You may continue reading the verdict."

"On the charge of cattle theft, we find the defendant, Will Gordon, guilty."

Mattie looked at her hands in her lap. She wasn't surprised. In fact, she felt a bit relieved. Her son would not steal from hard-working people ever again. She heard each of the boys' names mentioned with a verdict of guilty to the charge of cattle thieving. But all she could do was pray for Will.

Cyrus reached for her hand. She allowed him to comfort her. Mattie didn't want to look at him, though. This situation was hard enough to face. He squeezed her hand. The simple gesture of support brought unwanted tears to her eyes. She brushed them away.

"Will the defendants please rise?"

Will and his men rose to their feet in a singular motion. Holding her breath, Mattie stared at the back of her son's head.

The judge looked sternly at the boys. "It is the decision of this court that you all be hanged by the neck until dead. The sentence will be carried out five days from today on Saturday at noon. This case is closed."

A loud roar of applause erupted all around, drowning out the sound of the judge's gavel. Mattie fell against Cyrus. He wrapped his strong arms around her and held her tight. While others in the courtroom celebrated when they handcuffed the boys and led them out, their heads hanging low, Mattie's heart broke.

"Let's get you out of here," Cyrus said. He pulled Mattie to her feet and tugged her through the mob.

Mattie didn't know where she got the strength to move her feet. All she wanted to do was lie down and die from the grief wracking her whole being as the reality of Will's imminent death crushed her heart. Soon they broke through the huge door and out into the fresh air.

Cyrus attempted to say something to her, but she couldn't hear him through the din. He shook his head and continued to lead her down the street toward the edge of town. It didn't matter to Mattie where he took her.

One word replayed itself in her mind. *Hanged!*

The thought weakened her knees, and she felt Cyrus lift her off the ground. Her son would pay the ultimate price for his crimes. And Bob along with him. Jake. Mathew. Ernie. They all would be dead before the end of the week. Mattie heard herself sob, but felt nothing outside of her sorrow.

Hadn't God heard a word of her prayers? What would she do now? Was there anything she could do? She wanted to stay right where she was for the rest of her life. In Cyrus' strong arms.

She felt herself being carried. Her eyes remained closed while she cried into Cyrus' waistcoat. Then she felt herself falling. She opened her eyes and found herself being placed between the sheets on a downy bed. A flood of fresh tears rolled down her cheeks.

Cyrus brushed them away with a gentle touch. He kissed her forehead. Then he pulled up a chair and sat down beside her. A lady entered the room, carrying a cup.

"Here, drink this, dear," the woman said in a soothing voice.

Mattie obeyed and drank the warm liquid.

The lady smiled at her, then nodded to Cyrus. "She'll sleep better now," she said quietly. "I added some laudanum to help calm her."

Cyrus opened a Bible that lay on the night table and began to read. The comforting words calmed her troubled spirit and she soon gave in to sleep.

When Mattie awoke, the dim light from a single candle danced on the ceiling. She looked around the room and saw Cyrus, still sitting in the chair reading the Bible.

He looked up and smiled.

"How long have I been asleep?"

Cyrus opened his pocket watch. "About six hours. Mrs. Jodson gave you something to help calm you down and sleep."

Mattie suspected as much. "Where are we?"

"In my room at the boarding house. When you told me you've been camping outside of town, I figured you'd need the comfort of a bed, rather than the hard ground."

"Thank you." Tears threatened again. "What am I going to do, now? My only son…" She couldn't bring herself to finish the terrible words.

Cyrus nodded. "I know. And I'll be here for you through the whole thing. You can lean on me, Mattie." He paused, as if contemplating his next words. "I'm sorry for everything that's happened to you. I feel responsible, and know I can never make up for losing your son." His chin quivered and he clenched his jaw.

Mattie saw remorse in his eyes. "Cyrus, if you hadn't come along when you did, I might have had a few more years with Will. But it was inevitable he would be caught or killed. You had nothing to do with that. My son committed crimes and he is being punished." A sob left her throat. Cyrus quickly gathered her into his arms and held her to his chest. "What will I do now?"

He pulled her away from him and stared into her eyes. "You are going to go over to that jailhouse, and you are going to witness to your son about the saving power of Jesus. That's what you're going to do."

She blinked hard at him. Yes. Of course she would do that. She knew there was no use worrying about the future, when each day of this coming week would be the most crucial in her son's life.

"Thank you. You're right, Cyrus. I need to go over there."

"I think it can wait until you've had some supper. The boys are probably eating, too."

She nodded and preceded him out the door, following the delicious aromas down to the dining room. Several people were already seated at four tables in the room, and they immediately quieted when she entered. Feeling their stares, she headed toward a table with two empty chairs. Cyrus sat beside her.

Mrs. Jodson left her place and walked over to her, taking Mattie's hands in hers. "You're welcome in my home, dear. No charge. Any friend of Mr. Braydon's is a friend of mine. And considering what you've suffered through today…" She patted Mattie's shoulder. "We'll not talk about that right now. You eat some supper. You'll need your strength."

Mattie was grateful the chatty woman left them alone. Gradually, the dinner talk continued. Forcing herself to eat, Mattie finished quickly, then excused herself to get ready to go to the jail.

"Where are your things?" Cyrus asked when she exited his room.

"I don't have much left. It's all on the back of a dapple-gray horse down on a side street, two blocks from the courthouse. That is, if nobody robbed me yet."

"I'll walk downtown with you and bring everything back here.

Then I'll give you a ride home when you're finished. This town can be pretty rough at night."

"I'll be fine, Cyrus. And I wouldn't think of taking your room."

"I'm not letting you sleep out on the prairie while I stay in this luxury room." She saw the sparkle in his eyes and the gentleness of his smile. He may not love her, but he had a soft, caring nature.

"Thank you. I appreciate your kindness, Cyrus."

He nodded and escorted her out of the house and to the jail.

"Now don't you leave here until I get back," he commanded.

"Yes, sir." She turned to enter, but stopped. "Cyrus?"

He looked over his shoulder.

"Thank you again."

He smiled, tipped his hat, and walked down the boardwalk.

Mattie paused before entering the jailhouse. Would Will allow her to visit him? The thought hadn't occurred to her before. She took a deep breath and turned the doorknob. He was behind bars. She would have her say.

Chapter Sixteen

Mattie hated that her son, once tall, proud, and free, now sat on his bunk, dejected, deflated, and lost. He wrung his hands in his lap, staring at the dirty wall in the cell.

When Cyrus arrived to escort Mattie back to Mrs. Jodson's place, Will looked at him, his face void of expression. It tore at Mattie's heart. Five more days to reach him. She leaned over and kissed his cheek. Still no reaction.

"I'll be back tomorrow, son. I love you with all my heart. Always have and always will. Goodnight."

The deputy, who'd been sitting in a chair outside the cell, quickly stood to open the iron door for Mattie to let her out of the cell.

Cyrus escorted her outside. She breathed deeply. *Lord, please help me. I don't know if Will's listening. All I ask is that you soften my son's heart so that he will accept Your forgiveness for his sins and live with You in eternity.*

Mattie remembered her new resolve. As long as Will still breathed, there was hope for him.

She lifted her head and walked through the streets, her arm curled inside Cyrus'. If only he knew what being so close to him did to her, or how much she loved him. If only he would love her back. Mattie had never felt so alone and reviled as she did that moment. Rejected by her only son and unloved by Cyrus. Woodenly, she walked down the boardwalk, an empty shell devoid of the ability to function correctly.

Mattie clung to the tiny glimmer of hope piercing her heart. As long as Will remained alive, she could hope for him. Raising her head and watching a hawk soar overhead, she began to renew her trust in God for Will and for her future.

She knew God's promises would be there for her after this was over and she could rely on Him, but starting over at the age of forty-six frightened her. Being alone the rest of her earthly days wasn't a thought she relished. She would wake up each day and give it into God's hands. With His help, she hoped to make it through.

When they stepped onto the porch, Cyrus dropped her arm. "I'll be staying in the carriage house if you need anything."

"Thank you. You've already done so much for me."

He reached out and traced her jaw line. "I could spend my life doing things for you, and it would never be enough."

Her heart bounced in her chest. His words soothed the ache inside her. "Thank you." She turned and entered the house, leaving Cyrus standing alone on the porch.

Mattie prepared for bed. Looking in the mirror, she brushed her hair, and then she closely scrutinized her scarred face. It was healing nicely, and she'd soon look almost like herself again. She didn't think she looked her age. Did Cyrus think she was pretty? No. The sooner she prepared her heart for a life alone, the better off she'd be. There could be no more dreaming of Cyrus returning her love.

She tucked herself into bed, blew out the candle, and sobbed into the pillow.

The next morning, Cyrus sat with her at breakfast. How she loved his offer of strength during the most difficult time of her life. Yet, it didn't help her in starting her new life alone. The past six months had been nothing but contradictions, and she was tired of her heart being bounced around by circumstances.

When they finished eating, Cyrus walked outside with her. He directed her to the corner of the porch where a swing hung from the rafters, its whitewash faded from the sun and from obvious use.

"Sit down a minute."

Mattie stared at him.

"I want to pray with you. I recently read in the Bible where it says 'If two or more are gathered together in My name, there I will be in the midst of them'. With both of our prayers joining together, I think it will help."

She smiled and nodded. What a difference God has made in Cyrus' life. She was so proud of him for keeping on with his faith. They sat on the swing and bowed their heads, praying for Will's forgiveness. When they finished, Mattie took a deep breath. She felt peace.

"Thank you, Cyrus. I can't tell you how much I appreciate this."

"Maybe today will be the day Will comes to know his Maker." His smile matched the brightness of the sun.

Mattie tore herself away from the serenity and security of the porch, and Cyrus. The prayer bolstered her as she walked through the streets of Abilene on her way to the jailhouse.

Again, her son remained aloof and forlorn. She couldn't make him understand the gravity of dying without having forgiveness from God. But she didn't give up. He may not look at her, but he could hear her words. She knew the deputy guarding the cells also heard and fell asleep like so many people had back when she was younger and used to go to church regularly. How could she get through to Will?

Cyrus showed up at the same time a couple of young women arrived, pulling a cart with the noon meal for the prisoners. The deputy let Mattie out of the cell, and she walked out into the sunshine with Cyrus. The constant pounding of a gavel echoing in her ears reminded her of the short time her son had left on the earth.

It isn't supposed to be like this. This sort of thing doesn't happen to decent folk. Parents are supposed to go before their children. Mattie felt her knees give out. Strong arms caught her and pulled her to a bench in front of the hardware store. They sat together, Cyrus offering his handkerchief to her.

She didn't care if people stared at her. By now the whole town knew her to be Will Gordon's mother. After this was over, she'd never see any of them again. What did it matter to them that a mother's heart was breaking? None of them cared about her or her son.

Then she remembered Cyrus' strong arms holding her up. She had one good friend who apparently did care. The thought lifted her spirits and helped her gain control of her emotions.

"Let's go get something to eat," he suggested.

"I don't feel like being stared at today. I think I'll go back to the house for a while."

"Sounds like a good idea." He stood and helped her to her feet. They walked back to Mrs. Jodson's together in silence. Cyrus made her sit on the porch swing while he disappeared inside. He returned, wearing a smile that reminded her of when Will was a boy and had done something mischievous. The remembrance almost caused her to cry again.

Cyrus' smile disappeared and concern ruled his features. "It'll be all right. You'll see."

Mrs. Jodson came through the front door, carrying a tray. She set it down on a small table near the swing. "Enjoy your dinner." Then she went back into the house.

"I told her you didn't feel like eating in town. She figured it was such a nice day, you and I could eat right here on the porch."

"Thank you. That's so sweet of you both."

She plucked the napkins from off the plates of food and laid one across her lap. He handed her a plate and a glass of lemonade. They bowed their heads and Cyrus thanked the Lord for their food.

When finished, he tore into the ham on his plate. "How did it go this morning?" he asked between bites.

"Not well, I'm afraid. He isn't listening to me, even though I'm sitting right there beside him."

"Maybe he's mulling it all over. You know, like I did."

She hadn't thought of that. Will certainly had a lot to think about. How hard it must be to know one's life would soon end.

"You might be right. He's facing a lot for one so young. Maybe I'll give him some breathing room before I go back over there tonight." Her heart felt lighter than it had for some time. Hope. "He probably needs time to think about everything I've told him."

Cyrus nodded. "That's what I think, too."

When they finished their meal, Cyrus suggested a ride out of town. Mattie agreed. They saddled their horses and took off, leaving Abilene behind and the huge multiple gallows being built there.

It felt wonderful to Mattie to have the wind blowing through her hair, to gallop across the prairie, not thinking of anything but the freedom of the moment. By the time they got back to Mrs. Jodson's, much of the heaviness she'd felt the last two days had lifted from her.

It was with renewed energy and hope she stepped into the jail that night. Rather than preach hard at her son, she sat beside him, took his hand in hers and began reminiscing.

"I remember back when you were only eight years old and had to stay after school nearly every day that year." Will looked up at her as if she'd lost her mind. She ignored him.

"I never told you then, but a lot of times I couldn't help but laugh behind your back at some of your antics. Of course your father and I had to discipline you, but you sure gave us some good stories to tell." She laughed heartily, painfully aware that it was the only sound in the jail at that moment.

"I didn't know you and Pa laughed at me." Will chuckled and Mattie basked in the sound of it. "I guess if I'd have known that, I probably would have cut up even more."

"Yeah." Mattie sighed. "I did the best I could by you after your father died. I guess you needed him more than I thought."

Will reached an arm around her and pulled her close. "You were the best mother a kid could have." His voice broke. "I just wasn't a good son."

"Oh, but you are a wonderful son, dear. I couldn't have loved you more."

Will placed his other arm around her and pulled her tight to his chest. She heard a sob escape from deep within him. "I don't want to die, Mother," he whispered. "I'm so sorry to cause you all this grief. I'm so sorry."

They held each other and cried for nearly twenty minutes. The whole while, she heard her son whisper into her hair, now wet with tears. "I'm sorry, Mother. I'm sorry."

When their crying subsided, they continued to hold one another for another hour. Then Mattie heard the sound of someone clearing his throat loudly. She glanced over Will's shoulder.

The deputy's voice was subdued. " Time's up for tonight, ma'am."

"Thank you, sir." She kissed her son on both cheeks and stood to leave.

Will grabbed her hand. "You'll come again tomorrow?" The desperation in his voice cut through to her soul.

She smiled. "Nothing could keep me away."

As she exited the cell, Cyrus entered the jailhouse to escort her back home. As they were about to leave, Mattie heard Will's voice behind them. "Braydon?"

Cyrus and Mattie turned in unison.

"Thanks for looking after my mother. She's a pretty special lady, you know."

Cyrus nodded and smiled. "I know."

They left the building, Mattie feeling torn between her son's contrition and wishing for things that could never be. Her son would never know the love of a good, Christian woman. There would be no wife or children in his future. He'd said he was sorry tonight. That was a breakthrough. But was he willing to ask forgiveness of his Heavenly Father? Eternity was but a few short days away. How she longed to know she'd see him again in Heaven some day.

The next morning, Will gave Mattie all his attention when she visited him. They talked about days gone past, but not about the future. Mattie enjoyed being with him. He was the old Will once again, the one she knew before Cyrus came into their lives. She could never love her son more. She left that day feeling satisfied from just being in his company, laughing and sharing. There wasn't much more she could say to him about it. She'd read him every verse she knew on forgiveness. She'd witnessed about the transformation in her own heart. Yes, Will was in God's hands.

The next morning when she arrived at the jail, Will stood to greet her, his face beaming as brightly as the sunshine on the prairie. As soon as the deputy let her into the cell, he grabbed her off her feet and swung her around. She shrieked, and the deputy opened the cell and poked his gun at Will.

"It's okay, deputy. I'm not hurting her." Will laughed at the confused man.

"He didn't hurt me," Mattie confirmed.

The deputy shook his head and left the cell.

"What's got into you, son?"

"Mother, hold on to your bonnet, because you're not going to believe this."

Mattie's heart soared. Maybe they'd pardoned him. She'd heard of that happening. "What is it?"

Will looked in the direction of the deputy, who stared openly at them. He pulled her toward his bunk and they sat together, holding hands. Will faced her. "Last night after your visit, I couldn't sleep. You showed me how much you love me by just being with me." He lowered his voice, but his smile remained on his handsome face. "And I remembered you saying how God loves me even more than you ever could. So I started talking to Him under my breath. And next thing I knew I poured out my whole heart to Him."

Mattie began to cry. Was it true?

"And I did what you said I should. I asked Him to forgive me of my sins, and He did. I don't know how I know this, but it's true."

Mattie grabbed Will's neck and cried into his shirt collar until it was wet. "Thank you, Jesus."

"Mother, would you mind reading the Bible to me? I want to know more about what heaven will be like."

Mattie's hands shook as she took up her Bible and began reading. It didn't matter that what she read didn't have anything to do with heaven, Will would be there waiting for her.

Mattie and Will read the Bible the next two days, discussing what each story meant. Mattie answered his myriad of questions as best as she could. They talked about their past experiences together and about God.

Then, on the last night before his execution, Mattie entered his cell. His face was sullen, but he smiled at her when he took her hand and kissed her cheek. "Mother, I want to be alone tonight. I hope you understand, but I got to talk to Jesus."

Mattie felt her bottom lip begin to quiver. She tried her best to quench the tears that threatened to slide down her cheeks. Before coming into the cell, she'd determined not to let him see her weep.

"Mother, I love you more than words can ever say. These past few days have been the most wonderful I've had in a long time, thanks to you." He looked into her eyes in earnest. "Don't you see? I'm not afraid anymore. I want to spend my last night here in prayer. I've got so much to say to God."

Mattie nodded her head, afraid to trust her voice.

"Mother, I want you to promise to do something for me."

"Of course I will. What is it?"

"Don't come tomorrow. Leave town and never look back."

Mattie couldn't hold back her grief any longer. She fell against him and wept.

"I want you to remember me like I am right now. I've never been more alive, Mother. And I'm happy. The weight of my sin is no longer on my shoulders." He pushed her away so he could look into her eyes again. "Mother, I want you to hear what I'm saying. This is the best time of my whole life. I'm free. Can you understand that? And I want you to remember me this way. Promise me you won't be here tomorrow."

She nodded. "I promise."

"And there's one more thing…" He paused, the smile returning to his face. "When Cyrus Braydon asks you to marry him, I want you to say yes."

Mattie's mouth dropped open. "But he doesn't love me."

Will laughed, causing Mattie to feel a little foolish, although she wasn't sure what was so funny.

"Will held her face between his hands and spoke softly to her. "Believe me. He loves you more than you know. And I know you love him back." He nodded his head. "He'll ask you to marry him. And I want you to go with him. Be happy, Mother. Live a good, happy life. Do it for me."

She grabbed his neck, unsure what to say to that. But as his last wish, she couldn't turn him down, no matter how ridiculous it sounded.

"I will," she said weakly.

"I will love you for all eternity, Mother." He embraced her and squeezed so tightly, Mattie thought her ribs might crack.

"I will love you forever, too, son."

He broke their embrace and sent her out. She looked back one last time. Yes, he really was happy. And free. She memorized how he looked that moment, then turned and exited the jailhouse for the last time.

Knowing Cyrus wouldn't be by for another hour to get her, she decided to walk home without waiting for him. The night air smelled of sage. She walked down the boardwalk, bittersweet memories creating a sweet, gentle calm inside her.

God hadn't forgotten her. He heard her cries and saved Will from the eternal fires. She had a pleasant and satisfying picture of her son on his last night on earth. God had made him strong. Stronger than she thought possible. It was Will's strength in facing his toughest hour that gave Mattie the courage to go on.

She would live her life so as to make her son proud. Wherever that may be. When she arrived at the boarding house, she noticed the door to the carriage house open, and a light shone through. For some reason, she suddenly wanted to see Cyrus.

She stood in the entrance, and he looked up from where he was shining Mrs. Jodson's buggy. He dropped the cloth and polish and rushed to her.

"Is everything all right? I thought you'd be gone longer."

She smiled. Oddly, it wasn't forced, but the most natural thing for her to do this night. "Will wanted to be alone. He wanted me to remember him the way he was tonight." She had so much in her heart, she just had to tell someone. "He was so happy, Cyrus. And he was truly free. I can't explain it, but I know those bars no longer held him prisoner. It was as if he was already not of this earth, but he belonged in Heaven."

Cyrus came to her and stopped only a couple feet away. He leaned against the other side of the doorway. "Did he have any last request?"

Mattie held her breath. Dare she tell him what she promised her son as his last dying wish? She felt her face become hot and she looked away.

The silence remained a barrier between them.

Then Mattie remembered. "He asked me not to go to town tomorrow, but to leave and never look back. But I don't know where to go. I lived each day like there was no tomorrow, but I now find I have hundreds of tomorrows in front of me. I'm terrified."

"I have an idea where you could go."

Mattie raised her eyebrows. "You do? Where?"

Cyrus took a step closer. "I have this little place over in Waco. It's not much right now, but in a few years, it could be quite a gold mine."

"Thanks for the offer, but as good as a farm sounds to me right now, I'm afraid I'll need to live in a town so I can make a living. I figured I'd take in some sewing. And I could—"

Cyrus took another step toward her, nearly standing on her toes. He put his finger over her mouth. "Mattie, I'm not giving you a place to live. I mean, I am, but…"

She could smell the shaving soap he'd used that morning. "Then what were you offering me?"

"Me."

Mattie blinked in confusion for a moment.

Cyrus laughed quietly, his breath warming her face. "Mattie,

I'm asking you to marry me. I've loved you for some time now, and I want to take you away and make you happy all the rest of your days."

Mattie sucked in a breath and held it. Will was right. Cyrus loved her. But how had Will known? Her questions came to a sudden halt when Cyrus' mouth came down and pressed against hers. She froze. His hands touched her hair and each moment the kiss lingered, she felt herself melt more until she was a puddle in his arms.

"Marry me," he whispered against her cheek.

She remembered to breathe. Then she reached around his neck and hugged him tight. It had been the toughest year of her life. But God was restoring her life to her. Her plight was over. It was time to move on. She had a promise to keep.

Be happy, mother. Live a good, happy life. Do it for me.

Will had released her to carry on. She'd love him forever for that.

Thank you, son.

"I haven't heard you say it yet."

Mattie pulled away from Cyrus, but still held on to his neck. "I love you, too, Cyrus. And yes. I'll marry you."

~The End~

About the Author

Jeanne Marie Leach is a published author and freelance editor, who lives in the mountains of Colorado with her husband of 32 years and Nakiska, their Alaskan Malamute. She teaches classes to beginning writers and speaks on a variety of topics to women's groups.